Beverly, Right Here

Beverly, Right Here

Kate DiCamillo

CANDLEWICK PRESS

Copyright © 2019 by Kate DiCamillo

First edition 2019

Library of Congress Catalog Card Number pending
ISBN 978-0-7636-9464-7

19 20 21 22 23 24 LSC 10 9 8 7 6 5 4 3 2 1

Printed in Crawfordsville, IN, U.S.A.

This book was typeset in Joanna MT.

Candlewick Press
99 Dover Street
Somerville, Massachusetts 02144

visit us at www.candlewick.com

For Andrea Tompa

One

Buddy died, and Beverly buried him, and then she set off toward Lake Clara. She went the back way, through the orange groves. When she cut out onto Palmetto Lane, she saw her cousin Joe Travis Joy standing out in front of his mother's house.

Joe Travis was nineteen years old. He had red hair and a tiny little red beard and a red Camaro, and a job roofing houses in Tamaray Beach.

Beverly didn't like him all that much.

"Hey," said Joe Travis when he saw Beverly.

"I thought you moved to Tamaray," said Beverly.

"I did. I'm visiting is all."

"When are you going back?" she said.

"Now," said Joe Travis.

Beverly thought, *Buddy is dead — my dog is dead. They can't make me stay. I'm not staying. No one can make me stay.*

And so she left.

"What are you going to Tamaray for?" said Joe Travis. "You got friends there or something?"

They were in the red Camaro. They were on the highway.

Beverly didn't answer Joe Travis. Instead, she stared at the green-haired troll hanging from the rearview mirror. She thought how the troll looked almost exactly like Joe Travis except that its hair was the wrong color and it didn't have a beard. Also, it seemed friendlier.

Joe Travis said, "Do you like ZZ Top?"

Beverly shrugged.

"You want a cigarette?" said Joe Travis.

"No," said Beverly.

"Suit yourself." Joe Travis lit a cigarette, and Beverly rolled down the window.

"Hey," said Joe Travis. "I got the AC on."

Beverly leaned her face into the hot air coming through the open window. She said nothing.

They went the whole way to Tamaray Beach with one window down and the air-conditioning on full blast. Joe Travis smoked six cigarettes and ate one strip of beef jerky. In between the cigarettes and the beef jerky, he tapped his fingers on the steering wheel.

The little troll rocked back and forth—blown about by gusts of air-conditioning and wind, smiling an idiotic smile.

Why were trolls always smiling, anyway?

Every troll Beverly had ever seen had a gigantic smile plastered on its face for absolutely no good reason.

When they got to the city limits, Beverly said, "You can let me out anywhere."

"Well, where are you headed?" said Joe Travis. "I'll take you there."

"I'm not going anywhere," said Beverly. "Let me out."

"You don't got to be so secretive. Just tell me where you're going and I'll drop you off."

"No," said Beverly.

"Dang it!" said Joe Travis. He slapped his hand on the steering wheel. "You always did think that you was better than everybody else on God's green earth."

"No, I didn't," said Beverly.

"Same as your mother," said Joe Travis.

"Ha," said Beverly.

"You ain't," said Joe Travis. "Neither one of you is any better. You ain't better at all. I don't care how many beauty contests your mama won back in the day." He stomped on the brakes. He pulled over to the side of the road.

"Get out," said Joe Travis.

"Thanks for the ride," said Beverly.

"Don't you thank me," said Joe Travis.

"Okay," said Beverly. "Well, anyway—thanks."

She got out of the Camaro and slammed the door and started walking down A1A in the opposite direction of Joe Travis Joy.

It was hot.

It was August.

It was 1979.

Beverly Tapinski was fourteen years old.

Two

She had run away from home plenty of times, but that was when she was just a kid.

It wasn't running away this time, she figured. It was leaving.

She had left.

Beverly walked down the side of A1A. She had on an old pair of flip-flops, and it didn't take long for her feet to start hurting. Cars went zooming past her, leaving behind hot gusts of metallic air.

She saw a sign with a pink seahorse painted on it. She stopped. She stared at the seahorse. He was smiling and chubby-cheeked. There were a lot of little bubbles coming out of his mouth, and then one big bubble that had the words SEAHORSE COURT, AN RV COMMUNITY written inside of it.

Past the sign, there was a ground-up seashell drive that led to a bunch of trailers. A woman was standing in front of a pink trailer holding a hose, spraying a sad bunch of flowers.

The woman raised her hand and waved. "Howdy, howdy!" she shouted.

"Right," said Beverly. "Howdy."

She started walking again. She looked down at her feet. "Howdy," she said to them. "Howdy."

She would get a job.

That's what she would do.

How hard could it be to get a job? Joe Travis had done it.

After the Seahorse Court, there was a motel called the Seaside End and then there was a restaurant called Mr. C's.

MR. C'S IS YOUR LUNCH SPOT! said the sign. WE COOK YOU ALL THE FISH IN THE C!

Beverly hated fish.

She walked across the blacktop parking lot. It was almost entirely empty. She went up to the restaurant and opened the door.

It was cool and dark inside. It smelled like grease. And also fish.

"Party of one?" said a girl with a lot of blond hair. She was wearing a name tag that said *Welcome to Mr. C's! I'm Freddie.*

From somewhere in the darkness, off to the left, there came the ping and hum of a video game.

"I'm looking for a job," said Beverly.

"Here?" said Freddie.

"Is there a job here?"

"Mr. Denby!" shouted Freddie. "Hey, someone out here wants a job. Who knows why."

Beverly looked to the right, past Freddie. She could see a dining room with blue chairs and blue tablecloths, and a big window that looked out on the ocean. The brightness of the room, the blueness of it, hurt her eyes.

She remembered, suddenly, that Buddy was dead.

And then she wished she hadn't remembered.

"Forget it," she said out loud.

"Forget what?" said Freddie. "We're getting ready to close, anyway. This is just a lunch restaurant." And then she shouted again, "Mr. Denby! Hey, Mr. Denby!" She rolled her eyes. "I guess I have to do everything around here."

She walked off down the dark hallway. A minute later, she was back. A man with a mustache was walking behind her. There was a red crease on the man's forehead, and he had on a gigantic tie imprinted with little yellow fish.

"This is Mr. Denby," said Freddie. "He was asleep. Can you believe it?"

Mr. Denby blinked.

"He had his head down on the desk and everything," said Freddie. "He was snoring."

"I was not snoring," said Mr. Denby. "I was not sleeping. I was resting my eyes. Paperwork is hard on the eyes. Freddie says that you want a job."

"Yes," said Beverly.

"Well, we do need someone to bus tables. I'll have to interview you, I suppose."

"What's your name?" said Freddie.

"Beverly," said Beverly.

"I'll get right on it, Mr. Denby," said Freddie.

"You'll get right on what?" said Mr. Denby. He rubbed at the red mark on his forehead.

"You spell *Beverly* with a B, right?" said Freddie.

"Right," said Beverly.

"Follow me," said Mr. Denby.

The video game pinged and chortled. Mr. Denby headed down the dark hallway.

Beverly wasn't a big fan of following people.

But Buddy was dead.

What mattered now?

Not much.

Nothing really.

She followed Mr. Denby.

Three

The office smelled like fish and cigarette smoke. It had a big desk and three metal filing cabinets. The desk was piled high with stacks of paper. There was a fan balanced on one of the stacks.

"There's a lot of work to do around here," said Mr. Denby. He waved his hand in the general direction of the desk. "As you can see."

Beverly nodded.

"So I need someone with a good, strong work ethic," said Mr. Denby. "I need someone who believes in getting things done."

He reached out and turned on the fan.

The top layer of papers blew off the desk.

"Shoot," said Mr. Denby. "Do you see what I'm talking about here?" He turned the fan off and moved it to the floor. The papers fluttered and sighed. Mr. Denby sat down at the desk. He folded his hands.

"Sit down," he said. He nodded in the direction of an orange plastic chair. Beverly sat down.

Mr. Denby looked at her. "Let's see," he said. "Have you ever worked in a restaurant before?"

"No," said Beverly.

"Do you like fish?"

"Not really," said Beverly.

Mr. Denby sighed.

"I have three kids," he said. "Three girls. They're in Pennsylvania. With their mother."

Beverly nodded.

"It's a tragedy, having kids," said Mr. Denby. "Don't let anybody tell you any different." He stared at his hands. "What happens with kids is you want to protect them, and you can't figure out how to do it, and it drives you crazy. It drives you right out of your head. It keeps you up nights."

"Uh-huh," said Beverly.

She doubted that her mother had ever stayed up at night thinking about how she could protect anybody.

"How old are you?" said Mr. Denby.

"Sixteen," said Beverly.

Mr. Denby put his head down on the desk. And then he lifted it and looked at her. "Sixteen," he said. "I can't stand it." He put his head back down.

Freddie came into the office.

Mr. Denby raised his head again.

"Freddie," he said, "how old are you?"

"Why do we have to keep talking about this?" said Freddie. "I'm a high-school graduate. I walked across the stage and everything. Besides, you shouldn't talk to ladies about their age. It's rude. Here," she said.

She handed Beverly a name tag that said *Welcome to Mr. C's.* Underneath that was a piece of tape with white letters that said *I'm Beveryl.*

"Wow," said Beverly. "Thanks a lot."

"Making name tags is something that I'm just naturally good at," said Freddie. "Plus, I like using that little machine. It's like a wheel. You just find the right letter on the wheel, and you punch it down hard, wham, and a letter appears. It's like magic."

Mr. Denby said, "Margaret, Alice, and Anne. Those are the names of my girls. Someday one of them will go into a restaurant and lie to a man about how old she is. It makes me sad. But what can I do? What am I expected to do? I've got a business to run here. I've got mouths to feed. You can start tomorrow."

"But she's not waiting tables, right?"

"No, Freddie," said Mr. Denby. "She's not waiting tables. She'll bus tables. Have you ever bused tables, Beverly Anne?"

"No," said Beverly. "And my name is Beverly. Just Beverly."

"Right," said Mr. Denby.

"Anyone can bus tables," said Freddie. "Anyone can learn how to do that. It's not like it's a skill or anything."

"Great," said Beverly.

"It's not fun here," said Freddie. "You have to have a dream and work to keep it alive because it's not any fun at all doing this job."

"No one said it would be fun," said Mr. Denby. "It's a fish restaurant. Not an amusement park."

"Okay, well," said Freddie, "I'm only warning her."

"Good-bye, Freddie," said Mr. Denby.

"I'm telling you: you have to have a dream," said Freddie. She opened her eyes very wide.

"Good-bye, Freddie," said Mr. Denby again. He stood up.

Beverly stood up, too. "Thank you, I guess," she said.

"Sure," said Mr. Denby. He held out his hand. Beverly shook it.

"Come in at ten tomorrow," said Mr. Denby. "There's a lot to do. There's paperwork to fill out."

"Don't worry," said Freddie as Beverly was pushing open the door to leave Mr. C's. "He'll never find the paperwork. He can't find anything in that office. You can work here the rest of your life, and you'll never have to fill out any paperwork."

"I'm not going to work here the rest of my life," said Beverly.

"Ha-ha," said Freddie. "Tell me another joke. Better yet, tell that joke to Charles and Doris in the kitchen. This is the end of the road unless you have a dream."

Beverly opened the door.

Outside, the sun was so bright that it almost knocked her off her feet.

Four

So she had a job.

It didn't make her feel that much better.

She walked down A1A. She tried not to look behind her because the thing about Buddy was that he had always been behind her, and now he wasn't.

Up ahead, past Mr. C's, there was a phone booth. Beverly looked at it, glittering and flashing in the sun. She had the idiotic thought that what she should do was call Buddy.

Buddy.

Who was a dog.

Who had been a dog.

Buddy.

Who was dead.

She went up to the phone booth and pushed on the door and went inside. It felt like stepping into a tall, narrow oven.

Beverly pulled the door shut.

Her mother answered on the first ring.

She didn't sound too drunk.

"It's me," said Beverly.

"Where are you?" said her mother.

"It doesn't matter," said Beverly.

She heard the snick of a lighter. She heard her mother inhale.

"I just wanted to let you know that I'm okay," said Beverly.

"You're okay? That's what you called to tell me? That you're okay?"

"Yeah."

"Whoop-de-do," said her mother. "You're okay."

Beverly leaned her head against the glass of the phone booth. "I got a job," she said.

"Anyone can get a job," said her mother. "I've had a job my whole life, and you can see how much good it's done me. Where are you?"

Beverly said nothing.

"Fine," said her mother. "Don't tell me."

"I just wanted to let you know that I'm okay," said Beverly.

She hung up the phone.

She closed her eyes. She kept her head against the oven-door warmth of the glass. She could hear the cars going down A1A, and underneath that, there was the sound of the ocean — bright, hopeful, relentless.

Sweat was running down her face.

She kept her eyes closed for what seemed like a long time. When she opened them and lifted her head, she saw words glinting in the glass above her.

She read the words out loud: "In a crooked little house by a crooked little sea."

It was like the beginning of a story.

In a crooked little house by a crooked little sea.

She reached up and touched the words. Someone had scratched the letters into the glass with something sharp.

Beverly thought about Raymie.

Raymie was her best friend.

Raymie would like these words.

But Raymie — constant, reliable Raymie, Raymie who had never failed her — wasn't here, was she?

She was back there, back where Beverly's old life was.

Back where Buddy's grave was.

Beverly traced her finger slowly over the words.

How could a sea be crooked?

That was stupid.

She stood up straight. She opened the door to the phone booth. She started walking down A1A again, back the way she had come. She walked past Mr. C's.

She walked past the Seaside End Motel.

She walked to the Seahorse Court. The woman was still standing out in front of her pink trailer. She was still watering her stupid flowers.

She saw Beverly. She waved. "Howdy, howdy!" she shouted.

The woman was like something that would spring out of a cuckoo clock, shouting her stupid greeting on the hour and the half hour.

Beverly sighed. She turned down the seashell path and walked toward the pink trailer.

She couldn't say why.

"Howdy," she said when she was closer to the woman.

And then she said it again.

"Howdy."

Five

Hold up and let me turn off this hose," said the woman. "And then we can visit proper."

"I'm not visiting," said Beverly.

"Just let me turn this off," said the woman. She bent over and struggled with the spigot. "Well, shoot," she said. "My hands are so messed up with this arthritis that every little thing is hard to do sometimes."

"I'll do it," said Beverly. "Move out of the way."

The woman stood up, and Beverly bent over and turned the handle on the spigot.

"There you go," said the woman. She clapped her hands. "Easy as pie." She smiled. Her face was creased with wrinkles, and she had on a big pair of glasses that made her eyes look huge. She stared up at Beverly. She blinked.

"Now," said the woman. She blinked again. She looked like a baby owl. "I wonder who you belong to."

"What?" said Beverly.

"Who are your kin?" asked the woman.

Beverly shrugged.

"You don't have kin?"

Beverly shrugged again.

Joe Travis Joy was kin, she supposed. And there were all the cousins on her mother's side of the family. And her uncle.

And there was her mother, of course.

Even though Beverly didn't really feel like she was related to her mother.

And there was her father, who had been gone since she was seven years old.

She had a dog. Or she used to have a dog.

She had friends.

Well, one friend—Raymie.

Her other friend—Louisiana—had left and was in Georgia now.

It stunk, how people left.

"I don't have any kin," said Beverly.

She stared at the old lady. Either her hair was crooked or she was wearing a wig.

"Everybody has kin," said the woman in a very solemn voice.

Beverly was hungry and tired. She thought that she would like to sit down.

She felt as if she had traveled a long way.

Even though Tamaray Beach wasn't really that far from Lister.

She wished, suddenly, that she had gone farther.

"Listen to me," said the woman. She looked up at Beverly. Her glasses glinted in the late-afternoon light. "I think you're hungry. Now, am I right? Are you hungry?"

"Yes," said Beverly.

She was hungry.

The world got very quiet. There was no sound except for the ocean crashing and muttering.

It would be nice if the ocean would shut up for just a few minutes.

"You didn't tell me your name," said the woman.

Beverly looked down and saw that she had the name tag from Mr. C's in her hand. She held it up like it proved something.

"What's that?" said the woman. She leaned in closer. She squinted. "Bee-verl," she said. "Your name is Bee-verl?"

"It's Beverly. I just got a job."

"Over at Mr. C's?"

"Yes."

"Well, good for you. Although they do fry their fish half to death over there. I'm Iola. Iola Jenkins."

"Okay," said Beverly.

"Let me ask you something, Bee-verl."

"It's Beverly."

"I know it," said Iola. "I'm just joshing you. Now, here is what I need to know. Can you drive a car?"

"Yes," said Beverly.

"Well, now," said Iola. She cleared her throat.

"Here is another question. Do you enjoy playing bingo?"

"Bingo?" said Beverly.

"Never mind," said Iola. "Don't pay me no mind. Why don't you come on inside, and I will make you a sandwich?"

Beverly put the name tag in the pocket of her jeans. She followed Iola up a flight of crooked wooden stairs.

In a crooked little house by a crooked little sea.

"Now, you like tuna fish, don't you?" said Iola from up ahead of her.

What was it with people and fish?

"Sure," said Beverly.

"Good," said Iola. "I make the best tuna melt you will ever have in your life."

"Oh, boy," said Beverly. "I can't wait."

Six

"The thing about the Pontiac," said Iola when Beverly was sitting across from her at the tiny little table in the tiny little kitchen, "is that I promised my children I would not drive it. I signed a piece of paper, a—thingamajig."

"A contract?" said Beverly.

"That's it," said Iola.

Beverly picked up her sandwich and took a bite. It tasted like fish, but it also tasted good. Iola had toasted the bread and melted cheese on top of the tuna, and the sandwich was warm in Beverly's hands.

For some reason, she felt like she might cry.

She took another bite.

"I signed a contract," said Iola. "That's exactly what I did. It was Tommy Junior who made me do it. He's a lawyer. He had me sign it, and it says that I will not, under any circumstances, drive the Pontiac until further notice. Or some such."

"Why?" said Beverly.

"Why what?" said Iola. She blinked. Up close, her eyes looked even bigger and owlier.

"Why did he make you sign a contract?"

"Pshaw," said Iola. She waved a hand through the air. "It wasn't nothing much. I mixed up the reverse and the forward is all. I ended up driving the Pontiac into Bleeker's Insurance. I knocked a few bricks off the building — that's all, a few bricks. But my land! You would have thought that I had knocked the whole building down the way everyone went on about it.

"You know, those insurance companies deal with catastrophes all the time, and this was not a catastrophe. No, it was not—it was a few bricks. Ten, at most. And the front of the Pontiac got crumpled up some. It still runs! It's a wonderful car, and it still runs. But I can't drive it because I promised I wouldn't. Me, not driving! Why, I've been driving practically my whole life."

"I've been driving since I was in fourth grade," said Beverly.

"Fourth grade?" said Iola. She blinked.

"My uncle taught me. My mother was drunk all the time, and so he figured it was a good idea for me to know how to drive."

"For heaven's sake," said Iola.

Beverly shrugged. "All I'm saying is that I'm a good driver."

"The Pontiac is very large," said Iola. "It's a large car."

"It doesn't matter what size the stupid car is," said Beverly. "I can drive it."

When Beverly was done eating, they went outside to the carport.

The Pontiac was huge and olive-colored. Its front end was smashed in.

"Are you sure it still runs?" said Beverly.

"It runs," said Iola. "And I tell you what. I should just get in there and start it up and drive on out of here and go to the VFW on my own. I don't care about the contract. I don't! I'm happy to lie to the children. They lied to me all the time, growing up.

"But here is the truth: I'm afraid. I'm afraid of my own capabilities. I mean to say that I am afraid I've mislocated my capabilities." Iola sighed. "What it comes down to is that I don't know if I trust myself anymore."

"Give me the keys," said Beverly.

Iola went into the trailer and came back with the keys and a big black purse. Beverly got in the driver's seat, and Iola got in the passenger seat.

The Pontiac started right up.

Beverly backed it out of the carport.

"Well," said Iola, "you're good at backing up."

"I'm good at going forward, too," said Beverly. She put the Pontiac in drive, and they went down the little seashell road of the trailer park and out onto A1A.

Beverly smiled. She looked over at Iola. She was smiling, too. Her black purse was balanced in her lap.

Beverly went faster.

"Oh, my," said Iola. She put both hands on top of her purse. "Now, you have a driver's license, don't you?"

"Sure," said Beverly. She was only a year away from her learner's permit—less than a year, really. A learner's permit was a license, wasn't it?

She put her foot down on the gas. They went faster still.

This was what Beverly wanted—what she always wanted. To get away. To get away as fast as she could. To stay away.

Oh, I have slipped the surly bonds.

That was a line from a poem they had memorized in school.

Beverly didn't think the poem was that great, but she loved the words about the surly bonds, about slipping them. Those words made sense to her.

Iola cleared her throat. Beverly thought that she was going to tell her to slow down.

Instead Iola said, "Who do you belong to, child?"

"No one," said Beverly.

"Well, I don't believe that," said Iola.

"It's true," said Beverly.

"Where are you living?"

"None of your business," said Beverly.

But where was she living? She hadn't thought about that at all.

"When you get as old as me," said Iola, "everything is your business. How about I make you a deal?"

"I don't want to make a deal," said Beverly.

"The deal is you can stay with me. You can drive me to bingo at the VFW. And to the grocery store. We can help each other out until you're ready to go back to where you belong."

"You don't even know me," said Beverly.

"I do not," said Iola.

"I could be a criminal."

"Are you?" said Iola.

Beverly shrugged.

"My husband always did say that I was a fool

for trusting people. He said, 'Iola, you would trust the devil to sell you a pair of dancing shoes.'"

"Why would the devil be selling shoes?" said Beverly.

"The devil gets up to all sorts of nonsense," said Iola. "That's why he's the devil. But still—people got to go on their instincts sometimes, don't they? We got to trust each other in the end. Don't you think?"

Beverly could think of all kinds of reasons not to trust.

People leave—that was one of the reasons.

People pretend to care, but they don't, really—that was another one.

Dogs die, and your friends help you to put them in the ground.

That was a big one, right there.

"You can stay with me," said Iola. She reached over and patted Beverly's arm. "We will help each other out. We'll trust each other."

Seven

They stopped and got chocolate milkshakes at a place called Sandcastle Sweets, and when they came back to the Seahorse Court, it was dusk and a purple gloom was settling over everything.

Iola gave Beverly a nightgown to sleep in — one with pink flowers and lace at the collar.

Beverly thought that she would rather die than put it on.

And then she put it on.

She was making all kinds of questionable decisions: working at a fish restaurant, eating tuna melts, wearing flowered nightgowns.

"Do you know how to play gin rummy?" said Iola.

"Sure," said Beverly.

They went out to the small porch at the back of the trailer. There was a wicker couch out there, and a wicker chair and a little glass table.

Iola put a bowl of peanuts on the table, and then she dealt the cards.

"Don't hold back just because I'm an old woman and can't stand the thought of losing," she said.

"Why would I hold back?" said Beverly.

It was full dark outside.

A streetlight clicked on, and the little porch became a yellow island.

Beverly thought, *I have left home to wear a flowered nightgown and sit on a little tiny porch in a trailer park and play cards with an old lady. This is stupid.*

But where she had been had never truly felt like home.

Still, it was where Buddy was buried—out underneath the orange trees in the backyard. Beverly had dug the grave herself, crying the whole time and promising herself that once she stopped crying, she would never start again.

Putting dirt on top of his body—covering him up, sending him away without her—was the hardest thing she had ever done.

Raymie had come over to the house and stood with her in the backyard. She put dirt on top of Buddy's body, too.

"Buddy," Raymie kept saying. "Buddy, Buddy." She was crying. "How are we going to survive without him?" she asked. "He was the Dog of Our Hearts. That's what Louisiana always called him. Remember? How are we going to live without him?"

Beverly didn't know. She felt mad at Raymie for even asking the question.

"We should say some poetry," Raymie had said when they were done covering Buddy up.

Poetry seemed beside the point.

But Beverly had said the words she knew, the words she had been made to memorize, the ones about slipping the surly bonds.

And then Raymie had left, still crying, and Beverly had set off to Lake Clara, and, somehow, she had ended up here.

"What are you thinking about?" said Iola.

"Nothing," said Beverly.

"It's your turn," said Iola.

Beverly drew a card.

"Looka here," said Iola. "Here comes His Majesty, King Nod."

A fat gray cat stepped out onto the porch. He looked to the left and then to the right, and then he came running and jumped into Beverly's lap.

"Would you ever look at that?" said Iola. "Nod doesn't care much for people. He has truly only ever liked other cats. There used to be a Wynken cat and a Blynken cat, but they are both gone. And now Nod is left all alone."

"I don't like cats," said Beverly. She gave Nod a push, but he stayed where he was, purring.

"Listen," said Iola. "You can hear him. He sounds like a happy motor. Ain't that something? It's like he's been waiting on you to show up."

"Right," said Beverly.

The cat stayed in Beverly's lap until the last card game, and then right before Beverly won, Nod leaped up and left the porch with his tail high in the air.

Iola stood. She said, "Now, this here can be your room. This whole porch can be yours. I'll get you some linens."

She left and came back with flowered sheets and a flowered pillowcase, and a yellow towel and washcloth. Iola unfolded the sheets and spread them over the cushions of the couch.

"I can do that," said Beverly.

Iola tucked the sheets into the cushions. "I'm sure you can, darling. But right now, I'm taking care of you."

When she was done, Iola left the porch and turned off the light. "Good night," she said. "Sleep tight; don't let the bedbugs bite. And remember, tomorrow is bingo at the VFW."

"Oh, boy," said Beverly. "I can't wait."

She lay down on the couch. She pulled the top sheet up to her chin. It smelled like soap.

Bugs were hitting the louvers of the porch. She could hear the ocean breathing in and out.

Buddy was in the ground.

And Beverly was here. In Tamaray Beach. In a crooked little house by a crooked little sea. Wearing a flowered nightgown.

She would write to Raymie.

That's what she would do.

Tomorrow, she would ask Iola for a piece of paper and an envelope and a stamp, and she would write to Raymie and tell her about Mr. C's and about the phone booth words. She would tell her about driving the Pontiac. She would tell her about Iola and Nod.

She would say that she didn't know how they were going to live without Buddy. She would say that she didn't understand how they were going to survive, either.

Right before she fell asleep, Beverly saw Buddy's grave, the black emptiness of it. And then, sometime in the middle of the night, she woke up to Iola standing over her. She didn't have her glasses on. Or her wig. The top of her head was fuzzy. She looked like a baby chicken. She was standing there in the half-dark, and then she was gone.

Later still, the cat came in and curled up on top of Beverly's hair and started purring.

"Get off," said Beverly. She pushed at him, but all he did was purr louder.

Somewhere outside, a cricket was singing.

The cat purred. The cricket sang. The ocean muttered.

"Good grief," said Beverly.

She stopped pushing at the cat.

She gave in.

Eight

In the morning, Iola cooked Beverly an egg, sunny-side up. She made her toast. She cut the toast in half and buttered it. Beverly looked down at the blue plate with the toast and the egg on it, and the sentence that came into her head was "You can't make me stay."

She was getting ready to say those words out loud to Iola—*you can't make me stay*—when Iola said, "Remember, tonight is bingo at the VFW."

"You told me already," said Beverly.

"I'm reminding you is all. You play for money, and that makes it exciting. You could win as much as fifty dollars."

"Oh, boy," said Beverly.

Nod was up on top of the refrigerator with his back to them. His tail was hanging down, twitching back and forth like a metronome. He was staring at the wall very intently.

"What were you doing standing over me last night?" said Beverly.

"I wasn't standing over you, darling," said Iola.

"Yes, you were," said Beverly.

"You were dreaming."

"I was not," said Beverly.

Nod hopped down off the refrigerator and up onto the table.

"Shoo," said Iola. She waved her hand in the direction of the cat, but he just sat there, staring at Beverly and her egg.

The radio was on, playing a mournful orchestrated version of some Beatles song.

"I got an idea," said Iola. She sat down at the

table across from Beverly. "Why don't you and me trust each other like we said we would."

"I never said I would trust you," said Beverly.

"You didn't say you wouldn't," said Iola. She smiled.

And that was how they left things.

Beverly put on her same clothes from the day before. She pinned her name tag on her shirt. Iola said, "Good luck, Bee-verl!" and Beverly walked down the ground-up seashell road of the Seahorse Court and up to A1A. She walked past the Seaside End. She walked across the parking lot of Mr. C's and pulled on the door of the restaurant.

It was locked.

She had to knock on the door for a long time before Freddie came and opened it.

"We're closed," said Freddie. And then she said, "Oh, it's you. I forgot about you." She narrowed her eyes. "Weren't you wearing exactly the same outfit yesterday?"

"It's not an outfit," said Beverly. "And so what if I was?"

Mr. Denby came out of the office. He was wearing another big tie. This one had a single blue fish on it.

Mr. Denby pointed a finger at Beverly. "You look familiar," he said.

"You hired her," said Freddie. "Yesterday. She's busing tables. She's not waiting tables. She's busing them. And she has on the same clothes that she had on yesterday, which seems kind of gross if you ask me."

Mr. Denby snapped his fingers. "You're Beverly Anne," he said.

"Right," said Beverly. "I'm Beverly Anne."

"Let's get you an apron," said Mr. Denby.

The apron was long and green. It had a big C on the front of it. Mr. Denby put the apron over Beverly's head, and then tied it in the back. She could hear him humming. His breath came out in small gusts that smelled like toothpaste and fish.

"There you go," said Mr. Denby. He patted her on the shoulder. "You're all set. Freddie will show you the ropes. I'm going to head to the office and give my girls a call and wish them a happy Monday."

"Today's Tuesday," said Freddie.

"Thank you, Freddie," said Mr. Denby. He walked back to his office.

"Now," said Freddie. She turned and looked at Beverly. "What happens is I wait on the tables, and you pick up the dirty dishes and put them in the bucket, and you take the bucket back to the kitchen and give it to Charles, who washes the dishes. Also, you fill up water glasses sometimes, if there's not enough water in them. It's not complicated. But the guy before you sure thought it was. What was his name? I can't remember."

"Right," said Beverly.

"Listen," said Freddie. "I have to tell you that I might be a waitress right now, but I also have a real job—modeling with the Klezmit Agency, which is a really famous agency and everything. Right now, I'm modeling underwear, but the underwear job will lead to modeling clothing, and the clothes-modeling job will lead to Hollywood once a movie director sees me in a magazine. So, what I'm saying is that I will not be a waitress forever, and maybe you could be the Mr. C's waitress someday."

Beverly stared at Freddie.

"What?" said Freddie. "You don't believe me?"

"You model underwear?" said Beverly.

Freddie narrowed her eyes. She said, "What is your personal dream?"

"I don't have a personal dream."

"That right there is your mistake," said Freddie. "That is dead-end, one-road thinking. You have to engage in open-ended, multi-road thinking."

"Right," said Beverly. "Where's the bucket to put the dishes in?"

Freddie sighed. "Follow me."

They went through the dining room with its blue chairs and blue tablecloths and its window onto the blue ocean, and through a swinging door into the kitchen.

"Okay," said Freddie. "This is the kitchen. And that is Charles." She pointed at a short, broad-shouldered man wearing a green knit cap.

"Hey," said Charles. He looked up at Beverly and then down at the floor.

"Charles was a big-deal college football player," said Freddie. "But then something happened, right?"

"Tore my tendon," said Charles without looking up.

"Right," said Freddie. "He tore his tendon and now he washes the dishes, and that's the way life goes if you engage in dead-end, one-road thinking like I was just talking about earlier."

"Charles does a lot more than wash the dishes," said a gray-haired woman who was standing at the stove. "He does a whole lot of everything around here. Charles is indispensable. That's what he is. And Charles is getting back on his feet. Right, Charles?"

"Right," said Charles. "I guess."

"That's Doris," said Freddie. "She's the cook. She cooks the fish, so she thinks she's in charge." Freddie rolled her eyes. "Okay. Anyway. Charles and Doris, this is Beverly. She's going to bus tables."

Doris looked Beverly in the eye. Beverly stared back.

"Beverly," said Doris.

"Right," said Beverly.

"I had an aunt named Beverly. She was one smart cookie. You couldn't get nothing past old

- 47 -

Aunt Beverly. You be smart, too. Don't let this Barbie doll here lie to you."

"I haven't lied to her about anything," said Freddie. "I am a very truthful person."

"Make sure she tips out with you is what I'm saying," said Doris. "There needs to be some equity around here. Equity."

Doris turned back to the stove. It was stainless steel, and so was the sink and the table and all the counters and the gigantic walk-in refrigerator. Everything in the kitchen shone with a muted silver light. And Doris stood at the stove in her white dress and white shoes as if she were a queen and all of it belonged to her.

The back door to the kitchen was propped open with a cement block. Hot air was coming in from outside, and a seagull was standing right outside the door, looking in at them, cocking his head from side to side.

Doris turned from the stove and snapped a towel in the direction of the bird. "Get!" she shouted.

The seagull flapped his wings. He rose, and then

he settled back down in exactly the same spot and kept staring at them.

"Okay," said Freddie. "Anyway. Here are the buckets you use for busing. Like I said, you pick up the dirty dishes and put them in the bucket, and you bring the dishes back here and Charles washes them. That's how it works. It's not complicated."

"Yeah," said Charles. He looked over at Doris. "That's how it works. I guess."

"That's right," said Doris. "That's how it works. We don't get paid enough to make it work. But that's how it works for now." And then without even turning around, she shouted, "Get on out of here!"

Beverly wasn't sure who she was talking to.

But the seagull lifted both wings as if he intended to leave. He opened his mouth and closed it again.

And then he folded his wings and stayed where he was.

Nine

The lunch rush came in, and the kids screamed and threw fish sticks. They got up out of their chairs and ran into the little dark alcove where the video games were.

The video games pinged. They made noises of things exploding.

And the parents sat in the blue dining room and stared out at the ocean as if someone had cast a spell on them.

Beverly went from table to table with her bucket. She picked up people's plates and put the plates in the bucket. She took the bucket back to the kitchen and gave it to Charles, who took it from her and shook his head.

"No end to it," he said each time. "No end in sight."

The people became a blur, and the plates became a blur, and the noise and the cigarette smoke became a blur. It was all a loud, blurry dream.

But in a way, it was good because none of it left any room in Beverly's head for anything else. She forgot about Buddy. She forgot about his grave. She forgot about her mother. She forgot about Raymie. She forgot about the cat and the Pontiac and the flowered nightgown. She forgot about Iola and bingo.

She forgot everything.

There was nothing in her head but dirty plates and dirty forks and dirty napkins and people's loud voices; there was nothing but the weight of the bucket in her arms and the occasional bright flash of sunlight—light that bounced off the blue ocean and entered the blue dining room and made everyone cover their eyes and say, "Oooh, that is so bright."

Beverly's feet hurt and her arms hurt. She had ketchup on her jeans. She smelled like fish.

It was almost three o'clock and only a few customers were left when Mr. Denby said, "Come back to the office with me, Beverly Anne."

She followed Mr. Denby down the dark hallway to the office. The desk was still piled high with papers. The fan was on the floor, turning slowly from side to side, looking for something it had lost.

There was a safe in the wall. Its door was open.

When Beverly was a kid, she had seriously planned on growing up and becoming a safecracker. She had had a book on how to crack a safe entitled *The Safecracker's Manual*. She had read the book so many times that she had ended up memorizing parts of it, and she would go over the memorized parts in her head when she couldn't sleep.

Safes may be compromised surprisingly often simply by guessing the combination.

That was one of the sentences she had

memorized, and it popped into her head now as she stared at the open door of Mr. Denby's safe.

"I'm paying you in cash," said Mr. Denby, "at least until we get the paperwork filled out. And the paperwork can't be filled out right now because I can't seem to locate the paperwork. It's somewhere around here." He waved his hand at the desk. "I'm sure it's here. But in the meantime, I'm paying you under the table. Do you understand what I'm saying, Beverly Anne?"

"No," said Beverly.

"Good," said Mr. Denby. He handed her fifteen dollars. "You can come back tomorrow at ten. You hustled out there today. I appreciate that, and Doris and Charles appreciate that. I'm sure that Freddie appreciated it very much, too."

"Okay," said Beverly, even though she doubted that Freddie appreciated anything very much.

"See you tomorrow," said Mr. Denby.

Freddie was waiting for her when she walked out of the office. "Here," she said. She handed her two dollars.

"What's that for?" said Beverly.

"That's tipping out," said Freddie. "That's what that old grump Doris was so excited about. So next time you see her, tell her I tipped out, okay?"

"Okay," said Beverly.

"And one other thing," said Freddie. "Doris thinks she's insulting me when she calls me a Barbie doll. But it's not an insult. It's a compliment because Barbie is beautiful. Do you know I used to have a job as a Living Darlene?"

"Who's Darlene?" said Beverly.

"She's a doll, like Barbie, only not as famous. And prettier. Anyway, they hired me to be the living incarnation of Darlene, the Living Darlene, and I passed out coupons and so forth."

"Coupons for what?" said Beverly.

"Coupons for money off toys, okay? That was my first modeling job."

"Wow," said Beverly.

"Well, I'm not going to work at a restaurant for the rest of my life. I'm not going to end up like grumpy old Doris or broken Charles. I have dreams. I'm going to be somebody." She looked Beverly up and down. She said, "You could be somebody, too.

You've got good, long legs. How tall are you, any-way? Five eight? Five nine? It's good to be tall like that when you're a model. They want you to be tall. And your hair is nice. Let me see your teeth."

Beverly bared her teeth at Freddie.

Freddie took a step backward. "You're scaring me, kind of," she said.

"Good," said Beverly.

"Well, you should wear some different clothes tomorrow," said Freddie. "That's my advice to you."

"And you should mind your own business," said Beverly. "That's my advice to you." She pushed open the door to Mr. C's.

The sunshine hit her like a fist.

Here she was, Beverly Tapinski, alive in the world.

Ten

She left Mr. C's, and instead of walking down A1A back to the Seahorse Court, she turned and went behind Mr. C's, down to the water.

She walked over the sand, past the beach towels and plastic shovels and colorful umbrellas and the people who were spread out everywhere. She went right down to the water.

She took off her flip-flops and put them on the sand. She was getting ready to roll up her jeans, but then she thought, *Why bother?* She walked right into the water. First, it came up to her knees and then to her thighs, and then a wave came and tried to knock her over, and she let it.

She fell into the water. She rolled onto her back and stared up at the sky. She could see a tiny slice of moon suspended in the blueness.

Her father had brought her here, or to some beach near here, a long, long time ago, when a rocket was being launched into space. The two of them had left home when it was dark and gotten to the beach just when the sun was coming up.

They had sat together on the hood of the car. They had looked up at the sky. Her father kept saying, "Wait, wait. It will happen."

And it did.

The rocket went up.

The hood of the car had been warm. Beverly had been able to feel the engine cooling off, ticking underneath them like a gigantic heart.

Her father had held her hand.

And when the rocket finally went up in the sky, he had squeezed her hand so hard that it hurt.

Pretty soon after that, he left.

He went to New York and never came back.

He slipped the surly bonds.

Stupid poem.

Poetry was nothing but words to say over a grave, something to throw into a hole in the ground.

"Wynken, Blynken, and Nod," said Beverly out loud. That was a better poem. How did it go? She couldn't remember. Something about sailing off somewhere.

She would ask Raymie what the rest of the poem was when she wrote to her. Raymie would know.

Beverly floated on her back in the ocean and stared at the leftover moon, and then she swam to shore.

Her flip-flops were gone.

She walked through the sand and up to the hot pavement and down the side of A1A in her bare feet. She turned off A1A and walked down the seashell drive of the Seahorse Court.

Her feet felt like they were on fire.

Iola was out in front of the trailer, watering her stupid flowers.

"Lord, child," she said. "What have you been doing?"

"I went swimming."

"It certainly does appear that way," said Iola. She stared at Beverly. "Are you staying, then?" she said.

"I'm here," said Beverly, "aren't I?"

Iola laid down the hose and went into the trailer and got Beverly a towel. Beverly dried off as much as she could, and then she sat in the lawn chair in front of the trailer, directly in the sun. Her skin felt tight with salt water.

She closed her eyes and fell asleep and dreamed about the grave. She was standing over it, looking down into it, searching for Buddy. She couldn't see him. The hole was empty and deep, and in the dream, she thought, *Why did I dig the hole so deep?*

When she woke up, her clothes were dry and stiff, and the sun was lower in the sky. She and Iola drove to Discount Dave's, and Beverly bought three T-shirts and a pair of jeans and another pair of flip-flops.

Iola bought a toaster.

"I don't need a toaster," she said. "The one I got works just fine. But it's old. And this one is so new and shiny. Isn't it beautiful?"

"Yeah," said Beverly. "It's beautiful."

When they got back from Discount Dave's, Iola plugged in the new toaster and toasted some bread and made them both tuna melt sandwiches.

After they finished the tuna melts, it was time for bingo at the VFW.

And Beverly was still there, wasn't she?

She was still at the Seahorse Court with Iola Jenkins.

So she was staying.

She supposed.

For now.

Eleven

It turned out that you had to be eighteen years old to play bingo at the VFW.

"I'm eighteen," said Beverly.

"You show me the identification that proves it," said the old man at the door.

"She's my niece, Ralph," said Iola.

"I don't care who she's related to; she's got to be eighteen to play," said Ralph. "Them's the rules. It's a law, on account of gambling. Handed out by the government. And I ain't defying the government." Ralph had fingernails that were as yellow and thick as horns. His eyes were watery. He looked somewhere past Beverly when he talked.

"I don't need to play," said Beverly. "I didn't want to play to begin with."

"Oh, honey," said Iola.

"I'll wait in the car."

"Oh, honey," said Iola again.

"It's fine," said Beverly. "I don't care."

And she didn't care.

Who cared about bingo?

"Well, I can't let you wait in the car," said Iola. "It wouldn't be right."

"I'm going to wait in the car," said Beverly. "You go inside and play."

And before Iola could protest any more, Beverly turned and left.

The Pontiac was too hot to sit in. Beverly sat on the curb and stared up at the big VFW sign.

There was a bird's nest in the V. Sticks and grass were hanging out of the middle of it, and some small bird was going back and forth, adding things to the nest in a busy and important way.

Beverly thought about leaving. She had the keys

to the car. She could take the Pontiac and go. She could become a proper criminal—a car thief. Iola probably wouldn't even turn her in. She would just be sad and disappointed. Which was worse somehow.

So Beverly sat on the curb outside the VFW. She stared up at the sign. She watched the bird going back and forth.

And then the sign lit itself up. First, it made a humming and crackling noise, and then, one by one, the letters came to life.

V

F

W

Each letter was beautiful, and when Iola came out of the VFW, Beverly didn't get up off the curb. She just kept staring at the sign.

"There you are," said Iola.

Beverly said nothing.

"I won $18.50," said Iola. "And I had some fun, I suppose. But I was worried about you out here all by yourself."

"I'm fine," said Beverly.

"Well, $18.50 is enough for you and me to have a really good supper. Would you like some supper? We could get us some burgers and fries. What are you staring at?"

"There's a bird's nest up there," said Beverly.

Iola looked up. "I can't see it," she said.

"Well, it's there."

Iola stood and stared at the sign. Beverly could see the lit-up letters — smaller, less bright — reflected in Iola's glasses.

Beverly got up off the curb. She said, "Did you think that maybe I wouldn't be here when you came out? That maybe I would just take the car and go?"

"Well, sure," said Iola. She kept staring at the sign. "But I also figured that there was a real good chance you would be right here." She turned and smiled at Beverly. "And look at that. Here you are."

That night, Beverly told Iola "no, thank you" to the flowered nightgown. She slept in a T-shirt on the couch on the porch. The cat came in at some point and curled up behind her legs, purring.

When she woke up in the morning, Nod was gone, and Beverly's arms were sore from carrying the bucket full of dishes at Mr. C's. Her legs hurt, too.

She thought about the bird building the nest in the V at the VFW—flying back and forth and back and forth, and she thought about the lit-up letters, how beautiful they had seemed, how they had hummed in the darkness.

The smell of coffee wafted from the little kitchen.

Beverly lay on the wicker couch and looked at the gray light coming in through the louvers.

She felt as if something inside of her were humming, too.

Twelve

Iola was sitting out in front of the trailer in one of the lawn chairs. Nod was curled up in her lap.

When Beverly came outside, Iola said, "There's coffee in the percolator," but she didn't get up out of the chair.

Mist covered the bushes and the trees. Everything was muffled. But underneath the silence, there was the low, insistent mutter of the ocean.

"I get blue spells," said Iola without looking at Beverly. "You ever get them?"

"No," said Beverly.

"It's like somebody is setting right on top of my chest, to where I can't breathe or hope." Iola put a hand over her heart. "And then, after a time, it passes. It always does. I just have to wait it out."

Beverly nodded.

"I'm glad you're here," said Iola. "But I worry about you. You're too young to be away from home—I know you are. Surely someone is looking for you. But you give me comfort, and I can't help it—I'm glad you're here."

"No one's looking for me," said Beverly. "I'm going to get some coffee."

She went into the trailer and poured a cup of coffee and stood and stared out the little window, past the yellow curtains, and thought about how much she did not want to be a comfort to someone.

She went back outside with her cup of coffee.

A woman was standing in front of the trailer, talking to Iola.

"I see you got some company," said the woman, nodding in Beverly's direction.

"I do," said Iola.

"Now, who are you?" said the woman to Beverly.

The woman's hair was dyed bright red. She had on a green pantsuit, and she was smiling in a fake way.

"She's my niece," said Iola.

"I didn't know you had a niece," said the woman.

"Well, I do. And she is visiting me."

"Her hair is so dark. Is she some kind of Italian?"

"She's my niece," said Iola again.

"I'm her niece," said Beverly.

"All right. If you say so. The two of you don't look related at all. But there's no explaining some things, is there?" She smiled her fake smile. "Now, Iola, I'm heading out on a little walk. You let me know if you want to go to church this Sunday, and when it is that you want to go grocery shopping."

"My niece will take me grocery shopping, thank you very much."

"If that's how you want it," said the lady.

"That's how I want it," said Iola.

The woman walked away. Iola said, "That's Maureen. She's the one who's been taking me grocery shopping since I can't drive the Pontiac. But she won't ever take me to bingo. She says that bingo is corrupt. Corrupt and immoral! Have you ever in your life?"

"I don't like her," said Beverly.

"Me, neither," said Iola. "I never have. But lying to her about you being my niece cheered me up some. And it was nice to tell her 'no, thank you' for the grocery shopping. I hate grocery shopping with her. She won't buy one ding-danging thing unless she has some kind of coupon for it. She's cheap is what she is. My Tommy would have called her 'stingy of soul.' And that's exactly what she is. Stingy of soul."

"Her hair sure is red," said Beverly.

"She dyes it every week. The hair dye comes in a little box. She buys it at the store. With a coupon, of course. Do you want me to make you some eggs, honey?"

Even though Beverly wanted to say no, she said yes.

There was something about sitting at the tiny table in the tiny kitchen in the tiny trailer and having Iola slide a plate of food in front of her that made Beverly feel like a little kid might feel—happy, taken care of.

Maybe in her letter to Raymie she would describe Iola's kitchen—the yellow curtains and the tiny table and the blue plates and the clock that was in the shape of a cat, and how the real cat, Nod, sat on top of the refrigerator with his tail hanging down.

"Do you have a piece of paper and an envelope?" Beverly asked Iola.

"I do."

"I need to write somebody a letter," said Beverly.

"I figured," said Iola. "That's what them things usually add up to. Are you going to write home and tell them where you are?"

Beverly said nothing.

"Never mind," said Iola. "It ain't my business." She pushed herself up from the lawn chair. She made it halfway up and then sank back down. "That old arthritis is in my knees, too," she said. "Some days, everything hurts."

Beverly stepped closer. She reached out and

took hold of Iola's hand. It was bony and small.

Beverly pulled, and, slowly, Iola rose to a standing position.

"Oof," said Iola.

"Okay?" said Beverly.

"Okay," said Iola. She squeezed Beverly's hand. And then she kept hold of it as the two of them walked up the stairs and into the trailer.

Thirteen

Well, look at that," said Freddie. "You wore a different shirt today. It must be a national holiday or something." She was sitting at a table in the dining room, smoking a cigarette and rolling silverware up in blue paper napkins. Her hair was piled high on her head.

The sun flashed off the silverware. The room was empty except for Freddie and the mountain of napkins and another mountain of forks and spoons and knives.

Beverly stared at Freddie.

"What?" said Freddie.

"Nothing," said Beverly.

"I take it back about you being a model and all," said Freddie. "You might have good legs and good hair and white teeth, but you're not friendly enough. You've got to be friendly to model. People want to look at somebody that knows how to smile, someone who smiles like they mean it."

Freddie smiled a big fake smile.

"Like that," said Freddie. "That's how you do it." She stopped smiling, took a long drag off her cigarette, and blew the smoke up in the air.

Mr. Denby came out into the dining room. "Good morning, Beverly Anne," he said.

"Right," said Beverly. She went back to the kitchen.

Doris was at the sink, scrubbing something. Charles was mopping the floor.

"It occurred to me last night that you might not know what 'tipping out' means," said Doris without turning around, "what with you being young and wet behind the ears. Charles didn't know how things worked when he got here, either."

"I didn't know nothing," said Charles. "Still don't."

"You're learning," said Doris. "Now, Aunt Beverly, listen. Tipping out means that Barbie gives you a percentage of what she gets in tips. Ten percent, at least. How much did she give you yesterday?"

"Two dollars," said Beverly.

Doris snorted.

"What?" said Beverly.

"Pay attention to what's going on," said Doris. "See what people leave on the table. Know what things cost. Pay attention. Nobody watches out for you in this world."

"But you're watching out for me," said Beverly to Doris's wide, solid back, "aren't you?"

Doris snorted again.

Charles kept mopping the floor. He laughed a low laugh.

The lunch rush started slow, but by half past noon, Mr. C's was full of sunburned kids and dazed parents. Beverly was almost running with her bucket full of dishes, trying to keep up. Freddie was smiling her fake smile, moving from table to table. And Mr. Denby, wearing a tie with a frowning fish on it, kept escorting more people in.

The same thing happened that had happened the day before. Everything slid out of Beverly's head: Iola's bony, insistent hand; the memory of her father and the rocket launch; the VFW and the bird's nest; Buddy's grave and Raymie's question about how they were going to survive without him.

Beverly forgot. She didn't think. She just worked.

At one point, a fat old man with a cigar in his mouth pinched her on the butt.

"You're kidding," said Beverly, "right?"

"Sorry," he said.

"That's just Lou," Freddie told her. "If you don't complain about him, he tips more."

"Tips who more?" said Beverly.

Which shut Freddie up.

After lunch was over, Freddie gave Beverly two dollars.

"Is that my full ten percent?" said Beverly.

"What are you even talking about?"

Beverly stared at her.

Freddie rolled her eyes, and then she peeled three more dollars off a big roll of bills. "Are you satisfied now?" she said.

"Sure," said Beverly. "Thanks."

"Uh-oh," said Freddie. "Here comes Jerome. He's early."

A man was walking across the almost-empty dining room. He was big and dark-haired. He was wearing a red tank top and a thick gold necklace that winked in the light.

Freddie waved and smiled her model smile. "Hi, baby," she said. "Hi, Jerome. You're early."

"Who's the new girl?" he said, tipping his head in Beverly's direction.

Up close, Beverly could see that he wasn't that old—seventeen or eighteen, maybe. He had a toothpick in the side of his mouth. It waggled up and down when he talked.

"I told you about her already," said Freddie. "You never listen to me."

"I listen to you," said Jerome. "That's all I do—listen to you." He winked at Beverly. "Hi, new girl."

Jerome's shoulders were hairy, and his nose was big. He looked like a wolf in a cartoon. He reminded Beverly of her mother's boyfriends — stupid and desperate and sometimes mean.

"What's the matter, new girl?" said Jerome. "Cat got your tongue?"

"Beverly Anne," called Mr. Denby. He was standing at the threshold to the dining room. He looked tired.

Jerome took the toothpick out of his mouth and used it to salute Mr. Denby. "Good afternoon, sir!" he shouted.

"Hello, Jerome," said Mr. Denby.

"The world treating you okay, Mr. Denby?" said Jerome. He put the toothpick back in his mouth. He grinned. "How is the fish business, sir? Is it good?"

"The fish business is just fine, Jerome," said Mr. Denby. "Beverly Anne, if I could see you in the office?"

"Bye-bye, Beverly Anne," crooned Jerome as Beverly walked out of the dining room. "Bye-bye. Have a good time in the office with Mr. Denby, Beverly Anne."

Mr. Denby ushered Beverly into the office and closed the door. He turned to face her. He tugged at his fish tie.

"I don't like him," said Mr. Denby. "That boyfriend of hers is not good news." He sighed. "Of course, Freddie isn't exactly good news, either. She's a crackerjack waitress, though. Very motivated in that regard." He sighed again. "But I feel like she is primed to take a wrong turn. It's worrisome, how people can take a wrong turn and never right themselves. I hope that doesn't happen to you, Beverly Anne."

"Uh-huh," said Beverly.

"You think about these kinds of things when you're a parent," said Mr. Denby. "You do a lot of thinking about wrong turns when you're raising children. In any case, we're going to get the paperwork filled out just as soon as I locate the paperwork, but in the meantime, here is some cash. And I thank you for your good work."

"Thanks," said Beverly. She took the money.

"I'm guessing that you'll come back tomorrow?" said Mr. Denby.

"Sure," said Beverly.

"How's your grandmother?"

"I don't have a grandmother."

"I thought you said you had a grandmother."

"No," said Beverly.

"Well, maybe it's just that I saw you in the car with your grandmother yesterday."

"You didn't," said Beverly.

"Oh," said Mr. Denby. He gave his fish tie another tug. "My apologies. I wish for things to be a certain way, and that is how I see them. Wishful thinking, I suppose you would call it. It's a personality trait that drove my wife to despair." He sighed. "I have three daughters, you know."

"Yeah," said Beverly. "You told me."

"Right," said Mr. Denby. He clapped his hands. "I'm certain that I did. Well, have a good afternoon, Beverly Anne. Enjoy the sunshine. I will see you tomorrow."

"Sure," said Beverly. "See you tomorrow."

Fourteen

Beverly walked out of Mr. C's and saw a dark-blue pickup truck parked at a rude angle in the parking lot.

Jerome, she thought.

The driver's-side window was down. Beverly put her head inside the truck. It smelled like cigarette smoke and cheap cologne.

Yep. Jerome.

There was a gold graduation tassel hanging from the rearview mirror.

"Ha," said Beverly. "Right. I bet."

She opened the door of the truck, took the tassel off the mirror, and put it in the pocket of her jeans. She got out of the truck and slammed the door.

"Some people take a wrong turn and never right themselves," she said out loud.

The words cheered her up.

She walked across the parking lot of Mr. C's, and then turned down A1A going north, in the opposite direction from the Seahorse Court. Her arms hurt and her feet hurt. She smelled like fish and ketchup. She had a wad of cash and a graduation tassel in her pocket.

She decided that she wanted to buy something, but she didn't know what.

Up ahead, there was a sign for a convenience store called Zoom City. The word Zoom had wheels under it, and it was tilted to one side so that it looked like the letters were going somewhere in a hurry.

Out in front of Zoom City, there was a metal horse, the kind that you put a dime in to take a ride to nowhere.

Beverly had loved those horses when she was really little. And then she'd realized that she wasn't going anywhere—that the horse was always going to stay in the same place, no matter how much money you fed it.

She'd been three or four years old, standing out in front of the Tag and Bag with her mother, when she'd finally figured it out.

Her father was there, too.

"Get on the horse, Bevvie," said her mother.

"No," said Beverly.

"Get on the horse!" shouted her mother.

"The kid doesn't want to do it, Rhonda. Leave her alone."

"She loves these horses. Don't you love these horses, Bevvie? Every kid wants to get on a horse. That's what kids do. Get on the horse, baby."

"No," said Beverly.

"Get on the horse and have some fun!" shouted her mother.

But Beverly hadn't.

She wouldn't.

She didn't want to ride a horse to nowhere; she wasn't going to let herself get fooled.

"See how she is?" her mother said to her father. "Hard as a rock."

Beverly stared at the Zoom City horse. His mouth was open so that you could see his teeth. He looked terrified. But underneath the terror, there was sadness, too.

Beverly felt bad for him. It must stink sitting out in front of Zoom City, offering kids rides to nowhere.

Beverly patted the horse on his metal flank.

The door to Zoom City opened, and a woman came out dragging a screaming toddler.

"Stop it, Vera!" shouted the woman. "You can scream all you want, but you ain't riding the horse."

The kid didn't have on shoes or a shirt—just a diaper.

"Want to get on the horsie," wailed Vera.

"No," said her mother.

"Horsie! Horsie!" screamed Vera.

"Shut up," said the mother.

The door to Zoom City opened again. A boy came out. His face was red. He was wearing a name tag that said Zoom! Elmer.

"Here," he said to the mother. He handed her a dime. "Give the kid a ride."

He went back into the store.

"Horsie?" said Vera. She stopped crying.

"Get on the horse!" shouted Vera's mother. "The nice man gave you a dime, and now you need to get on the horse!"

Vera blinked. She opened her arms so that she could be picked up.

"Go ahead," said the mother. "You want it so much, get on there your own self."

"Stop it," said Beverly to the mother. "Can't you just stop it?"

She knelt. "Come here," she said to Vera. She held out her arms.

Vera stumbled over to her, and Beverly picked her up. The kid smelled like pee and talcum powder. She was as solid as a sun-warmed brick in Beverly's arms.

"I wonder what you think you're doing," said the mother.

"I'm putting the kid on the horse," said Beverly. "Duh."

"Horsie," said Vera.

"Right," said Beverly. "Okay. There you go. Do you know how to hold on?"

Vera nodded. "Yes," she said. Her face was streaked with snot and tears. She grabbed hold of the reins.

"Okay, then," said Beverly. She turned to the mother. "Put the dime in, would you?"

"Who do you think you are?" said the woman.

But she dropped the dime in the box, and the horse started to move. Vera held on to the reins and looked up at Beverly.

"Horsie go," she said in a wonder-filled voice.

"Sure," said Beverly. "Horsie goes. Right."

She turned away. She opened the door to the store.

Fifteen

The boy named Elmer was behind the counter. He was holding an oversize book with wings on the cover of it.

The wings were a bright, impossible, glorious blue.

"What are you reading?" said Beverly.

Elmer slowly lowered the book and looked at her. His face was still red. Acne. Lots of it. His eyes were a brownish gold.

"It's a book," he said.

"Yeah," said Beverly. "I thought so. What's it about?"

"Italian Renaissance art," he said. "Any more questions?"

"Yeah. Is your name really Elmer?"

"Why wouldn't it be?"

"I don't know, maybe because Elmer is an old man's name. Or the name of somebody who hunts rabbits and doesn't ever catch them."

"Maybe I am an old man," said Elmer. "Maybe I'm ten thousand years old. Maybe I've been living in this convenience store for the last thousand of those years. In addition, maybe I hunt rabbits. Maybe I catch them and strangle them with my bare hands." His acne-covered face was getting redder. "But if I'm a ten-thousand-year-old rabbit hunter, I'm not going to tell you about it, am I? I would be a myth, a superhero. I would be a scientific marvel. And I wouldn't waste my time talking to you, would I?

"If you're here to buy something, you should buy it. If you're in here to ask questions, then the question-and-answer session is over. Because I'm not participating anymore. Got it?" He gave her a long look. And then he raised the book so that it covered his face.

"Wow," said Beverly. "Okay."

She turned away from the counter. She walked down the aisle. Her heart was beating fast. She felt like she had been running.

She looked around her. Toilet paper. Beef jerky. Corn chips. Windshield-wiper fluid. A baseball cap that said *Alligator Meat*.

What did that even mean?

Outside Zoom City, Beverly could see that Vera was still on the horse. At least you got a lot of time for your dime, even if you did end up in exactly the same place you started.

Beverly stood and studied the candy section: Red Hots, licorice whips, gum. She grabbed two pairs of wax lips and took them up to the counter.

"You're buying wax lips?" said Elmer. He slammed his book shut. "Nobody buys wax lips."

Beverly studied the blue wings on the cover of the book. They belonged to an angel who was hovering over a woman with her hands on her cheeks. The woman didn't look all that happy.

But then, neither did the angel.

"Well?" said Elmer.

"They're a gift," said Beverly.

"Some lucky person's going to be overjoyed."

"I saw what you did with the girl and the horse."

"Yeah?" he said. "What did I do?"

"You gave her a dime."

"What's your point?"

"My point is that you're sitting here reading a book about art and angels, and you give dimes to little kids who want horse rides. You pretend like you're tough, but you're not tough."

Elmer's face was getting redder.

Beverly handed him a dollar. "The other thing your name makes me think of is glue," she said. "We used Elmer's glue all the time in grade school. I got in trouble for eating it. I think that's why I ate it. I ate Elmer's glue even though I didn't really like how it tasted. It was just a way to piss the teachers off. Anyway, it occurred to me that maybe you were telling the truth. Maybe you are a ten-thousand-year-old man who hunts rabbits and kills them with his bare hands, but then maybe what you do is glue the rabbits back together with Elmer's glue, because, like I said, you aren't tough at all. And you feel remorseful about what you did to the rabbits. Maybe that's who you are."

Elmer stared at her.

He was smiling, but also trying not to smile.

His face was very, very red.

Beverly picked up the wax lips and said, "You can keep the change." And then she walked out of Zoom City without looking behind her.

Those were the most words she had said to anybody in a long time. It could be that they were the most words she had ever said to anybody at one time in her whole life.

It was possible.

She looked down at the wax lips in her hand.

Something inside of her was fluttering, turning. She felt like there was a bird trapped in her stomach, flapping its wings.

She walked down to the ocean and threw Jerome's graduation tassel into the water. It floated there for a minute, looking like some exotic sea creature, and then it disappeared, borne out to sea on a retreating wave.

"Good-bye and good luck," said Beverly.

She stood and stared at the water for a long time.

Finally, she turned and headed back to the Seahorse Court.

Sixteen

Iola was out in front of the trailer, sitting in a lawn chair. Nod was in her lap. His tail was hanging down, twitching back and forth.

"Here," said Beverly. She handed Iola a pair of wax lips.

"Thank you, darling," said Iola. She turned the lips over in her hand, looking at them. "What are they?"

"Lips," said Beverly.

"What do I do with them?"

"You do this," said Beverly. She put her pair of lips in her mouth, over her own lips. The wax was sweet and thick.

Iola looked at her and laughed. "Have you ever in your life?" she said. She put her lips on and held very still. Her eyes were huge behind her glasses. She looked like a little lost owl with a very big mouth.

Beverly laughed.

Iola spit the lips out. She said, "I have never before heard you laugh."

Beverly shrugged. She took the lips off. She said, "I guess I've never heard you laugh, either."

Iola put the lips back on. Beverly couldn't help it—she started to laugh again.

She could still feel the bird inside of her, flapping its wings. She thought about Elmer. She thought about the angel on the cover of the book, and about the wings on the angel.

She had never seen anything so blue in her life.

She hadn't known a blue like that existed.

Beverly could smell the ocean. She could hear

it. Suddenly, things seemed good and possible in a way that they hadn't before.

Iola let out a whoop of laughter, and Nod leaped out of her lap and stalked away, tail high.

A door banged. Maureen came out of her trailer and walked toward them, her red hair flaming and her arms crossed over her chest.

"Yoo-hoo," she said. "Is everything all right over here?"

"Yep," said Beverly.

Iola kept the wax lips in her mouth. She nodded.

Maureen looked at Beverly. She said, "Who are you, anyway? You're no relative of Iola's. Seems to me that you are just some con artist trash."

Whatever had been inside of Beverly flapping its wings stopped and held very still.

Beverly stared at Maureen. She said, "I've got an idea. Why don't you shut up."

Iola took the wax lips from her mouth. "This child is my niece," she said.

"I don't believe that for a second," said Maureen. "I'm going to call Tommy Junior and tell him something funny is going on over here."

"Don't you dare call Tommy Junior," said Iola. "I can run my own life. I don't need Tommy Junior telling me what to do. This child belongs to me. She is my kin. And that's all there is to it."

"We'll see about that," said Maureen. She turned around and walked back to her trailer.

"Well, shoot," Iola said after Maureen disappeared. "And here we was having so much fun. Help me up," she said, holding out her hand to Beverly.

Beverly pulled Iola out of the chair.

"Do you want me to leave?" said Beverly. "I could stay someplace else."

"I do not want you to leave," said Iola. "I ain't going to let Maureen bully me. And besides, where would you go?"

Beverly shrugged.

"Do you think that's who I am?" Beverly said. "Con artist trash?"

"No," said Iola.

"You don't know who I am," said Beverly.

"That's not true," said Iola. "I know exactly who you are." She looked at Beverly, and then she nodded and walked past her, up the steps into the trailer. She turned and said, "Come on inside and let me make you a tuna melt. It will give me an excuse to use that new toaster." She smiled.

Beverly didn't say anything.

"Come on, now," said Iola. "It will be fine. Everything will be fine."

"I'll be there in a minute," said Beverly.

She sat down in the lawn chair.

It will be fine. Everything will be fine.

She wasn't sure, but she didn't think that anyone had ever said those words to her before.

Beverly looked down at the wax lips in her hand. They were misshapen now, starting to crumble.

She thought about how she should probably write that letter to Raymie.

In a crooked little house by a crooked little sea. It will be fine. It will be fine.

Everything will be fine in the crooked little house by the crooked little sea.

Right.

Seventeen

Hey," said Jerome the next day when he came to pick up Freddie. "Hey, Beverly Anne. You seen my graduation tassel?"

"Your *graduation* tassel?"

"Yeah, it's missing."

"Why would I know anything about your stupid graduation tassel?" said Beverly.

"It's just that I meet you, you leave, and then I go out to my truck, and guess what?" Jerome took the toothpick out of his mouth and studied the tip of it closely.

"What?" said Beverly.

"Well," said Jerome. He put the toothpick back in his mouth. "I go out there, and my tassel is gone. I meet you, and my tassel disappears. That's a— what do you call them things?"

"A coincidence?" said Beverly.

"Yeah," said Jerome. "A real strong coincidence."

"What color was it?"

"Huh?"

"Your graduation tassel. What color was it?"

"Gold," said Jerome.

"Gold like you were an honor grad?"

"Yeah," said Jerome. "Gold like that."

"Well, if I find your gold honor-grad tassel, I'll let you know."

"Beverly Anne!" called Mr. Denby. "Could you please see me in the office?"

"Yeah, Beverly Anne," said Jerome. He took a step closer to her. He smelled like sweat and cologne. "Why don't you go and see Mr. Denby in the office? Huh? Why don't you sit down beside him and help him count out all his money?" He winked at her.

"Beverly Anne?" said Mr. Denby again.

Beverly walked away.

It was satisfying to think that Jerome's stupid tassel was probably halfway to Cuba by now.

After Mr. Denby paid her and said that he was going to locate some paperwork for her to fill out very soon, Beverly went to Zoom City. She walked there without really planning to do it. She told herself she wanted to see the horse.

And the horse was right where she had left him—bolted in front of the store, his mouth open and his teeth showing, that look of terror and sadness in his eyes. Stupid horse. She touched his flank. It was warm from the sun.

The Zoom City door opened. Elmer stuck his head out and said, "What? Do you need a dime?"

"No," said Beverly. "I don't need a dime."

"There's no age limit, you know," said Elmer, waving his hand in the direction of the horse. "Anyone can ride."

"Ha-ha," said Beverly. She looked at his face,

at the mask of pimples, his heavy-lidded eyes. He stood with one foot in Zoom City, and the other foot outside. His name tag was on crooked.

Elmer.

Who named their kid Elmer?

"Quit looking at me," Elmer said.

"I'm not looking at you," said Beverly.

"Right," he said. "Sure, you're not." Suddenly, he stood up straighter. He looked past Beverly. "Good afternoon," he called out. "Good afternoon, Mr. Larksong."

Beverly turned.

An old man with a cane was walking across the parking lot, picking his way slowly through the spangled brightness of pop tabs embedded in the macadam.

"Hello, Elmer," the man called back.

Elmer pushed the door open wider. He smiled. His teeth flashed. They were straight and even and white.

"I'm going to purchase some cigarettes today, Elmer," said the man, when he got closer to them. "Today's the day. Don't try to talk me out of it."

"Stevie's not here, Mr. Larksong. And I won't sell them to you. I just won't. So, no cigarettes for you, I guess." He smiled. "In any case, I don't think that cigarettes are the answer."

"What is the answer, then?"

The old man stood next to Beverly. He was breathing heavily. There was a peach-colored hearing aid in his ear. It looked like a misshapen seashell—something that you would pick up off the beach, look at, and then throw back into the ocean.

"Maybe you know what the answer is," Mr. Larksong said, turning and looking at Beverly.

"Nope," she said. "I don't."

He smiled at her. He had false teeth.

"Who's your young friend, Elmer?" said Mr. Larksong. "I like her. I like anybody who doesn't claim to know the answers."

"I'm not his friend," said Beverly.

"She's not my friend," said Elmer.

"Got it," said Mr. Larksong. "Not friends." He smiled again. "Let's try it this way, then. What's your name, young lady?"

Beverly stared at Mr. Larksong. He stared back

without blinking. He had eyes like a lizard—tiny and bright.

"All right, then," he said. "I'll go first. I'm Frank. Frank Larksong. Larksong, as in *The Song of the Lark*. Ever seen that painting? *The Song of the Lark?*"

"No," said Beverly.

"It's a beauty," said Mr. Larksong. "Makes you stop and listen." He coughed. He cleared his throat. "Yep," he said. "That's me. Frank Larksong. And you are?"

Beverly said nothing.

"Look," said Elmer. "Never mind. Who cares what her name is? I don't know her name, and I don't need to know it. Why don't you come inside where it's cool, Mr. Larksong?" Elmer stepped back and held the door wide.

"Come on," said Elmer. "Inside."

Mr. Larksong smiled his big denture-filled smile at Beverly, and then he walked past her, leaning heavily on his cane, and went inside Zoom City. But Elmer kept standing there, holding the door open. He wasn't looking at Beverly. He was staring somewhere past her.

"Well?" he said.

Beverly could feel the cool air from inside flowing out.

She could hear the ocean.

"Well, what?" she said.

"Hurry up," said Elmer, still not looking at her.

She shrugged. She stepped past him.

She went inside.

Eighteen

Mr. Larksong stood up at the counter and talked to Elmer, and Beverly walked up and down the aisles of Zoom City, looking at the toilet paper and baseball caps and beef jerky and packages of gum. She pretended that she had come in for something and wasn't finding it—whatever it was.

Chips, antifreeze, paper towels, masking tape, aspirin, milk, hard candy, soft candy, knit hats, key chains.

Why was there so much crap in the world?

Up at the counter, Mr. Larksong kept coughing. He would say something to Elmer and then cough. Every time he coughed, he put both his hands on the counter, as if he were working to push the counter deep into the ground.

"What are you looking for?" Elmer called to her.

Beverly thought about the blue wings on the angel on the front of Elmer's book.

That was what she was looking for—that brilliant, impossible blue.

How stupid was that?

"None of your business," she said to him.

"Come up here, young lady," said Mr. Larksong. "I want to show you something."

Beverly rolled her eyes.

She walked slowly up to the front of the store. There were three oversize books open and spread out on the counter, their glossy pages shining in the fluorescent light.

"This," said Mr. Larksong, jabbing his finger at one of the open pages, "is *The Song of the Lark.*" He started to cough. But he kept his finger where it was, pointing at a painting of a girl standing in a field. The girl was holding a scythe. The sun was coming up behind her. Even without the sun being all the way up, there was light everywhere.

"I don't see a lark," said Beverly.

"Exactly," said Mr. Larksong. He put both hands on the counter and coughed again. "It's called *song of the lark*."

Beverly stared at the girl in the painting. She didn't have any shoes on. You could tell by the way she held her body that she was listening.

"You can't paint a picture of a song," said Beverly.

Mr. Larksong smiled at her. "But he did it anyway, didn't he? The painter painted a song without painting a musical instrument, without even painting a bird." He closed the book. "Elmer is going to learn all about that."

"I told you," said Elmer. "I'm not going to study art. I want to be an engineer."

"Going to Dartmouth," said Mr. Larksong to Beverly. "Sixteen years old and he's got a full scholarship." He slapped his palm on the counter.

"That's the kind of boy you're dealing with here." He coughed.

Elmer looked down at the counter. His face was getting redder.

"In the meantime," said Mr. Larksong, "I'm dying. Cancer. Lung cancer. Cigarettes will kill you. You don't smoke, do you, young lady?"

"No," said Beverly.

"Good for you," said Mr. Larksong. "Okay, well, I guess I'll be on my way. Elmer, it was good to see you. And, you," he said to Beverly, "whoever you are, I hope to see you again."

Mr. Larksong leaned on his cane and made his way slowly over to the door.

"Good-bye, Mr. Larksong," said Elmer.

Mr. Larksong pulled the door open wide. It closed slowly behind him.

"Are all of these books yours?" said Beverly.

"Library," said Elmer.

"Where's the one with the angel?"

"What?" said Elmer. He looked up at her. "Which one with the angel? Art is filled with angels."

"The one you had yesterday," said Beverly. She

could feel her own face getting red, but she kept going. "The one with the Italian Renaissance art." The words felt strange and sharp in her mouth.

Elmer reached under the counter and pulled out another book.

"This?" he said.

The blue of the angel's wings was just as astonishing as it had been the day before. And the angel looked just as annoyed—like she had too much to do and no one was helping her get it done.

The Zoom City door opened, and a man with a baseball cap and sunglasses came into the store. He was whistling.

"It's called *Annunciation*," said Elmer. "What do you like about it?"

Beverly said nothing.

"The painting," said Elmer. "Why do you like it?"

"Who said I liked it?" said Beverly. And then she said, "Because of the wings."

Elmer nodded.

"My name's Beverly," she said.

"What's your last name?"

"Tapinski."

He stared at her.

"What?" she said. "Do you want to know my middle name, too?"

"Sure," he said.

"Louise," said Beverly. "Satisfied?"

"I'm Elmer."

"Yeah, I know."

"I'm reminding you," he said. And then he raised the book up so that it covered his face. "I get off at five," he said from behind the book. "In case you were wondering."

"I wasn't wondering," she said.

But Beverly Tapinski was smiling when she left Zoom City.

Nineteen

She wasn't going to wait for Elmer to get off work.

She wasn't.

But she didn't want to go back to Iola's. And she didn't want to go to the beach. She walked to the phone booth. She stood and stared at it without going inside.

She thought about her mother, sitting on the back porch, drinking beer and smoking cigarettes and staring out at the scraggly orange trees, resenting them.

"Those lousy trees. They can't grow one piece of fruit that isn't sour. I should cut them all down."

But she never did cut them down.

Buddy was buried under those trees.

He was alone with no one but her mother to watch over him.

Which was the same as no one at all watching over him.

Beverly went into the phone booth and picked up the phone, but she couldn't make herself dial.

What would she say?

Rhonda Joy Tapinski, could you please, just for once, help me out?

Could you watch over Buddy?

Ha.

Buddy was dead.

And Beverly's mother didn't watch out for anybody but herself.

Beverly hung up the phone. She thought about the annoyed angel with the blue wings. She wished she could send her to go and stand over Buddy's grave, or float over it, or whatever it was that angels did. Hover? Flutter?

She leaned her forehead against the glass, put her hand up above her head, and felt the words. They were still there. Of course they were.

In a crooked little house by a crooked little sea.

She could read them without even seeing them. She liked that. She ran her fingers over the words again and again.

And then she pulled open the door to the phone booth and stepped outside and looked up at the sun. It was at least four o'clock. Elmer got off at five.

Who was she kidding?

She turned. She went back to Zoom City.

She sat down in front of the mechanical horse. She leaned her head up against his flank and closed her eyes.

"Now, I'm just wondering if I can be of some assistance to you," said a voice.

Beverly opened her eyes. A lady in a green wraparound skirt was bending down, smiling at her. The wraparound skirt had ducks on it, hundreds of them.

"Are you lost?" said the woman. "Weary?"

"I'm not lost," said Beverly.

"Are you weary?"

"I'm fine," said Beverly.

"Yet here you are, sitting all alone on a summer's day." The woman stood up. She put her hands on her hips and beamed at Beverly. Her hair was gathered up on top of her head in a big brown pile. There was a pencil stuck in the top of the pile. The late-afternoon sun was visible behind the woman's left shoulder — a smoldering ball of light.

"Can I interest you in salvation?"

"What?" said Beverly.

"Salvation," said the woman.

Beverly sat up straighter.

"Here," said the woman. "Take this." She held out a piece of paper. "Take it. It tells the truth."

The door to Zoom City opened. Elmer stuck his head out. "Mrs. Deely?" he said.

"What?"

"I told you. You can't do that."

The woman turned and looked at Elmer. "Do what?" she said.

"Harass people."

"I'm not harassing anyone. The truth has been

delivered to me, and I'm delivering it to others. How can that be harassment?" Mrs. Deely looked confused.

"It's fine," said Beverly. "I don't care."

"See?" said Mrs. Deely to Elmer. And then she turned back to Beverly and held out the paper again. "I made it myself. Read it at your leisure. You will know it to be true."

"Thanks," said Beverly. She took the paper and looked down at it and saw that it was covered in little stick figures with balloons coming out of their mouths. There were tiny words in the balloons.

"It's a cartoon," said Mrs. Deely. "To make the truth more accessible. I drew it myself. Under divine guidance."

"Okay," said Beverly.

"Good-bye, Mrs. Deely," said Elmer.

"Good-bye, good-bye," said Mrs. Deely. "I will pray for you." She waved at both of them, and then she walked around the side of Zoom City, past the hedge, down toward the ocean.

"What are you doing out here?" said Elmer.

"Waiting," said Beverly.

"For what?"

"For you," said Beverly. "Duh."

Elmer smiled. He looked down at his feet. "I'll be off pretty soon," he said.

The door to Zoom City closed.

Beverly leaned back against the horse. She looked at Mrs. Deely's cartoon. There were so many words crammed into each balloon that it was almost impossible to read anything. One of the stick figures was screaming; at least, Beverly assumed it was screaming. Its mouth was open in a big, agonized O. And there was another stick figure that looked like it was getting consumed by fire.

Also, there were a lot of snakes. The stick figures were holding snakes in their hands and waving them around. They were jumping up and down on snakes. And there was one really big snake. Or maybe it was an alligator; it had feet. The creature, whatever it was, had a bubble over its head. Beverly squinted. "And the truth shall be delivered to you in fire and dim gladness." Those were the words inside the bubble.

"Good grief," said Beverly out loud.

She folded up the paper and put it in her back pocket.

She closed her eyes again. Iola was probably wondering where Beverly was. She was maybe thinking that Beverly wasn't coming back. She was probably standing out on the front steps of the trailer, looking up the road, waiting and hoping for Beverly.

It was terrible—how people waited for other people.

Beverly couldn't stand it. Talk about fire and dim gladness. She didn't want to think about it.

She took Mrs. Deely's cartoon out of her back pocket and looked at it again.

One of the stick figures was standing on top of a mountain with both arms over its head. There was a bubble coming out of its mouth, but there weren't any words inside the bubble.

Did Mrs. Deely forget to put the words in?

Or was the stick figure trying to say something that couldn't be said in words at all?

Twenty

She hides in the bushes," said Elmer. "And then she kind of leaps out of the bushes and pounces on people and makes them take those cartoons. It scares them."

"I wasn't scared," said Beverly.

"Yeah, well, that's you. She draws cartoons of people dying and getting burned up in fires and consumed by snakes, and then she gives the cartoons to kids when they're sitting on the horse. It makes the kids cry. They think that since it's a cartoon, it's something fun. And it's not fun. There's no point in scaring people. Life is scary enough as it is."

They were walking down A1A, side by side. Elmer had a book bag slung over his shoulder, and Beverly was close enough to him that her arm kept brushing against the canvas of the bag.

"Where are we going?" she said.

"To the bus stop," said Elmer.

They walked past the phone booth.

"Wait," said Beverly. She stopped. "I want to show you this."

"Yeah," said Elmer. "It's a phone booth. I've seen it before."

"No," said Beverly. "Inside."

"What?" said Elmer. "Is Superman in there?"

"Ha-ha," said Beverly. She pulled open the door. "Go inside."

"You go first," said Elmer.

"Good grief," she said. "You don't trust anybody, do you? Fine." She stepped inside. "Look.

Here I am. Inside. Nothing has happened to me."

Elmer put down his book bag. He stepped inside, too.

"It stinks in here," he said.

Up close, Elmer's face was cratered, angry, covered in pimples.

"I feel like Hansel," said Elmer. "I feel like I just got shoved into the oven by the witch."

"Tilt your head," said Beverly.

"What?" said Elmer.

"Look up," she said. She pointed.

"Oh," said Elmer. "Words."

"Read them," said Beverly.

"In a crooked little house," said Elmer, "by a crooked little sea."

Beverly's heart thumped. It was strange, almost painful, to hear someone else say the words. It was as if Elmer were reading something that had been written inside of her, carved into her.

He said the words again, faster this time. "In a crooked little house by a crooked little sea. That's good," he said. "I like it."

"Did you write it?" said Beverly.

"Me? No. I don't write poetry. Let's get out of here. It's too hot."

They stepped out of the phone booth. Elmer picked up his book bag. "I've got a question for you," said Elmer.

A truck blew past them, blaring its horn.

"Okay," said Beverly.

"What did you like about the wings? In the painting?"

"They're so blue," she said. "I've never seen a blue like that."

Elmer nodded.

"How did they do that?" she said.

"Do what?"

"Make that color."

Elmer stopped walking. He looked at her. "It's a gem," he said. "It's lapis lazuli. They ground it up and turned it into paint."

"Lapis lazuli," said Beverly.

"Right," said Elmer. He started walking again.

"Lapis lazuli," she said quietly to herself.

It was like muttering a spell, an incantation.

And then they were at the bus stop. Elmer looked at his watch and said, "The bus should be here any minute now."

"Where's Dartmouth?" said Beverly.

"New Hampshire."

New Hampshire. Which was, what? A thousand miles away?

"So you're going to be an engineer?"

"Yeah, I hope so."

Cars rushed past them in a hot, metallic blur. Suddenly, Beverly couldn't stand the world—its heat and noise and violence, how all it ever wanted to do was to strip things away.

"I hate everything," she said.

"How old are you?" said Elmer.

"What difference does that make? I'm fourteen."

"Right," said Elmer. And then the bus came, and Elmer was climbing the steps. He turned back and said to her, "Lapis lazuli. That's one thing you don't hate. And me, right? You don't hate me." He smiled at her. "I'll see you tomorrow, okay?"

"Right," said Beverly. "Okay."

She stood and watched the bus pull away. She

couldn't see Elmer inside, but she stood there and waved anyway.

What was wrong with her?

Waving at a person she couldn't even see.

Waving at a bus like some little kid.

"Lapis lazuli!" she shouted after the bus. "Lapis lazuli!"

They were such beautiful blue words.

She couldn't help it. She loved them.

She waved until the bus disappeared.

Twenty-one

She went back to the Seahorse Court. Iola wasn't in the front yard. Beverly walked up the little steps and knocked on the door.

She waited. She knocked again. The door opened, and there was Iola — big-eyed, unsmiling.

"Hi," said Beverly.

"Hi?" said Iola. "That's what you're going to say to me? Hi?"

"I guess so," said Beverly.

"I've been waiting for you for I don't know how long," said Iola.

"I didn't ask you to wait for me."

"I even put those lips on," said Iola, "and I just sat here and waited for you, thinking how it would make you laugh if you come up the drive and seen me sitting here with those waxy lips on my face. And when you didn't show up, I just ended up eating them."

"How did they taste?" said Beverly.

"Terrible!" said Iola. "Waxy. And not near sweet enough."

Beverly stood on the steps, and Iola stood in the doorway.

Somewhere behind them, the ocean was muttering.

"Don't wait for me," said Beverly. "I can't stand to think about you waiting for me."

"I waited," said Iola. Her glasses slipped down her nose. She pushed them up with one finger. "Just because you can't stand to think about something don't mean it ain't happening, that it ain't true. People wait on other people. People rely on other people."

Iola's glasses slipped down again, and again she pushed them back up.

The glasses looked bigger than they had the day before. It was like Iola was shrinking.

Nod came and squeezed through Iola's legs. He went down the steps and into the yard, his tail high.

Iola stood at the door without moving.

Beverly didn't move, either. She just stood there. The ocean kept muttering. The sky was turning some kind of ominous pink. But then, pink always looked ominous to Beverly. It made her think of princesses and beauty contests and her mother and lies.

"Well," said Iola.

"Well," said Beverly. "Are you going to let me in?"

"I'm always going to let you in, darling," said Iola. "It's not a matter of whether or not I'm going to let you in."

Nod stood at the bottom of the steps and looked up at the two of them. He made a noise that sounded like a question. The sky above the trailer turned from pink to purple. Dark clouds were rolling in.

"That cat wants to come back inside now," said Iola. "In, out, in, out. You can't ever predict what a cat wants."

"I made a friend," said Beverly.

"What?" said Iola.

"I made a friend."

"Oh, honey," said Iola.

Beverly shrugged. "His name is Elmer. It's a stupid name. He works at Zoom City."

"Oh, honey," said Iola again. "I'm so glad."

Nod came bounding up the steps. He wound himself through Beverly's legs, working to trip her. She could hear him purring. The sky was dark with clouds now. "You stupid cat," said Beverly.

"It's fixing to rain," said Iola. "Come on, now."

She took hold of Beverly's hand, and Beverly bent down and picked up Nod.

They went into the trailer that way—the three of them together.

Iola immediately set to work making Beverly a tuna melt. How was it that Beverly hated fish and worked at a fish restaurant and ate tuna fish every day of her life? How had that happened?

Rain was beating hard on the roof of the trailer. Beverly sat down at the little kitchen table and saw that there was a piece of paper placed right in the center of it. The paper was white with a border of little purple flowers, and there was an envelope with little purple flowers sitting on top of the paper. And on top of the envelope, there was a pen. The envelope had a stamp on it.

"What's this?" said Beverly.

"Well, what does it look like?" said Iola. She fussed with the toaster.

"Stationery," said Beverly.

"That's right," said Iola. "You said you wanted to write a letter, and I forgot about getting you what you needed. And then I remembered, and now there it is. Right in front of you."

Nod leaped up on the refrigerator. He put his back to them. He studied the wall as if it contained some great mystery. His tail swung back and forth. Maybe someday, Nod would solve the mystery. Maybe a door would slide open in the wall, and

Nod would leap through it and not come back.

But for now, he was here.

Beverly picked up the pen.

Dear Raymie, she wrote.

She sat still for a minute. She listened to the rain.

And then she bent her head and wrote:

There is this phone booth here that is just kind of on the side of the road, but also not very far away from the ocean, and someone has scratched some words inside it, on the glass. I don't know who did it, but I guess that doesn't matter.

What I wanted to tell you is that if you don't know to look for the words, you could miss them. You could end up not seeing them at all. The thing is that you have to turn your head just the right way.

Don't worry. I'm going to tell you what the words are. There's a lot I'm going to tell you. But first, I want to ask you a favor.

Could you go and visit Buddy's grave?

Beverly wrote for a long time. She used both sides of the paper. She had to ask Iola for another piece, and she still wasn't anywhere near done.

She sat in the crooked little kitchen by the crooked little sea and wrote and wrote.

Twenty-two

You're getting good at busing tables," said Freddie. "You could even wait tables if you wanted. I mean you should think about it someday. At some different restaurant. Not here. Because I am the waitress here."

"Yeah," said Beverly. "I know."

"What I mean is you should think about dreaming bigger. You should think in a multi-road way. I took a seminar about all of that once. It was called 'Dream Big,' and that was what they taught you. To dream big and drive on lots of roads and not to ever settle. And right after I took the seminar, I got the job as a Living Darlene, and I could see that my destiny was coming true."

"What destiny?" said Beverly.

"The destiny of becoming famous," said Freddie.

"Right," said Beverly.

The two of them were in the dining room of Mr. C's, rolling silverware up in napkins. Freddie was smoking a cigarette.

Beverly was sitting with her back to the ocean. She couldn't see it and she couldn't hear it, but she could feel it back there, heaving itself up and down, glittering.

"Jerome dreams big. I mean, he didn't take the seminar or anything. He didn't need to. He just kind of does it naturally. He's going to be rich someday."

"Good for him," said Beverly.

"Jerome knows a lot," said Freddie.

"I bet he does," said Beverly.

"Look," said Freddie. She tilted her head back and blew cigarette smoke up in the air above their heads. "You can be all snotty if you want to. What

I'm saying is that you have to have a dream. If you want to get stuck here busing tables for the rest of your life, then go right ahead. Be my guest. You and broken Charles and grumpy old Doris and Mr. Fish Manager will be very happy together, I'm sure."

Mr. Denby came walking toward them. He was smiling a big smile and wearing a tie with a green octopus on it. Beverly couldn't tell for sure, but it looked like the octopus had nine legs.

"Freddie," Mr. Denby said, still smiling, "do you think it's a good idea to smoke as you roll the silverware?"

"Yes," said Freddie. "I do."

"I've been thinking," said Mr. Denby. "What we need to do around here is smile more, all of us."

"I smile a lot," said Freddie.

"We're in the hospitality business, after all," said Mr. Denby.

"I thought we were in the fish business," said Beverly.

"I've noticed that if you smile a lot, people will tip you more," said Freddie. "Can I just point out that Doris and Charles don't ever smile?"

"They're not in the front of the house," said Mr. Denby.

"And also," said Freddie, "I guess they just don't have that much to smile about."

"Right," said Mr. Denby. He ran his hand over his head. He smoothed down his octopus tie. He cleared his throat. "Yes," he said. "Okay, well, I'm ready to open the door. Freddie, put out the cigarette and let's start the show."

"What show?" said Freddie.

"The fish show," said Beverly. "Duh."

At the end of her shift, Beverly was waiting for Mr. Denby in the office. She was sitting in the orange chair. The fan had disappeared. Two of the cabinet drawers were ajar. The paper piles on the desk looked bigger.

The safe door, as usual, was open.

Beverly stood up and walked over to the safe and looked inside. There were several piles of bundled-up twenties and lots of loose pieces of paper.

Beverly picked up a stack of twenties. She could

take it. She could take it without even cracking the safe. It would be easy.

She put the money back.

And then she saw a photograph.

Its edges were curled.

Beverly picked it up.

The photograph was of Mr. Denby. He was wearing a Santa hat. There was a baby in his lap, and the baby had on a Santa hat, too. And there were two little girls in green dresses with red bows, sitting on the floor in front of Mr. Denby. Next to Mr. Denby was a woman, also wearing a Santa hat.

Everyone in the photo was smiling.

They were sitting in front of what looked like a fake Christmas tree. There was a window behind the tree, and you could see outside to the real world. Snow was falling—fat white smudges of it were visible against the glass of the window. And there was a tree outside. It was leafless, and its branches were black.

Mr. Denby looked happy. He wasn't wearing a fish tie. The oldest girl had a missing front tooth. She was smiling biggest of all.

Beverly slid the photo into the pocket of her jeans, and then she sat back down in the orange chair.

Mr. Denby came whistling into the office a few minutes later. "Beverly Anne," he said, "I am very proud of the work you are doing. And at some point, we will get that paperwork filled out and make everything official here. But for now, please take this little bonus and my grateful thanks."

He handed her two tens and a five.

"Thanks, Mr. Denby," she said.

And then as she walked past the kitchen, Freddie handed her a wad of singles. She said, "Here. Tell Doris that I tipped out."

"I don't care what you do!" shouted Doris.

Beverly said, "Thank you, Doris."

"What are you thanking her for?" said Freddie. "I'm the one who gave you the money."

"Something around here needs to change!" Doris shouted. There was the crash of a pot being slammed down. "There needs to be equity. I'm not kidding. I'm tired of it."

"I have no idea what she's talking about," said Freddie.

"She's talking about equity," said Beverly.

"I don't know what that means," said Freddie.

Another crashing sound came from the kitchen.

"Equity means that things should be equitable, just," said Beverly.

"Just what?" said Freddie.

"Never mind," said Beverly. "I'll see you tomorrow."

She went out the front door of Mr. C's and into the bright light of late afternoon. Jerome was walking toward her, which was too bad because the day had been pretty good up to that point.

"Hey, Beverly Anne," he said, "I saw you and your boyfriend yesterday, walking down the road."

"Sure you did," said Beverly.

"Yeah, I blew my horn and all. But you two were too much in love to notice."

Beverly stared at him.

Jerome smiled. "I know that guy. Your little boyfriend. He was in my algebra class. What's his name?" Jerome knocked on his head with his fist. "Let me think. Oh, yeah. I got it. Fudd. Elmer Fudd."

"Why don't you shut up?" said Beverly.

"Yeah," said Jerome. "Fudd. You think I don't know things, but I do. Beverly Anne and Fudd sitting in a tree, K-I-S-S-I-N—"

Beverly pushed past him.

"G," said Jerome. "Hey, do me a favor and tell Fudd that I said 'hey.' Tell him thanks for all the help in algebra class."

He drew out the word *algebra*. He said it as three distinct words.

Al. Gee. Bra.

"And any time you want to give me back my graduation tassel," said Jerome, "here I am. Waiting." He spread his arms out wide. "I know it was you who took it, Beverly Anne."

She turned away from him and walked across Mr. C's parking lot. Her heart was pounding hard. She marched down A1A. Cars flashed past her in a hot river of sound.

Beverly walked faster. She got to Zoom City, yanked open the door, and walked inside.

Elmer was behind the counter, reading from a book called *American Art from A to Z*. The picture on the front of the book showed a diner with people sitting inside. The painting was green. Everything and everyone in the picture looked green and lonely.

What was the point of painting green, lonely pictures?

"Hey," said Elmer. He lowered the book and smiled at her.

"You didn't tell me that you know Jerome," said Beverly.

"Who?"

"Jerome," said Beverly. "You helped him in algebra?"

Elmer's face went from red to white. He put the book down on the counter.

The Zoom City door opened, and Mr. Larksong came in. "Good afternoon, all," he said.

"Do you?" said Beverly. "Know him?"

"Know who?" said Mr. Larksong.

"Jerome," said Beverly.

"Who's Jerome?" said Mr. Larksong.

"Yeah, Elmer," said Beverly. "Who's Jerome?"

"Okay," said Elmer. He held up his hands, and then put them down carefully on the counter. "Let's see. Who's Jerome? Jerome is the person who pulled my gym shorts down to my knees in PE every day. My shorts and my underwear. Because it was funnier that way, if my underwear came off, too. But, wait—that's not right. It wasn't every day. Because it was more fun for Jerome if some days he did it, and some days he didn't. That way, I could be terrified in between, waiting for it to happen, anticipating it. And that was so much fun! Man, Jerome knew how to have a good time."

"Hold up," said Mr. Larksong. "What is this? What are you kids talking about?"

"Also," said Elmer, "Jerome is the person who put duct tape over my mouth and wrapped duct tape around my body and duct-taped me to a chair. Duct tape! Isn't that original? Huh?" Elmer was talking faster now, jamming his words together. "Who's Jerome? I'll tell you: he's the person who used his profound imagination, his deep-thinking skills, to duct-tape me to a chair and lock me in the janitor supply closet. Guess how long I stayed in there? Half a day. Half a school day. Mr. Jerowski, the janitor, found me. That was funny, too, when the janitor found me. Because he yelled at me in Polish. And ha-ha-ha, what's funnier than a janitor yelling at a duct-taped boy in Polish? Nothing."

Elmer looked right at Beverly. His face was a splotchy red. His hands were still on the counter. They were shaking.

"Okay," she said.

"No," said Elmer. "It's not okay. Because, remember? There was algebra. I 'helped' Jerome in algebra. And that means that Jerome copied my algebra homework every day. I did it wrong sometimes. On purpose. I got an F just so he would get an F. But it didn't make any difference. Nothing made any difference. Because it was Jerome, and that was the way things were."

Beverly could hear Mr. Larksong breathing next to her, his lungs wheezing.

"So, yeah," said Elmer. "I know Jerome. So what? I know Jerome."

"Well," said Mr. Larksong. He coughed. And then he reached up and fiddled with his hearing aid. "That's quite a story. If I heard it right."

"I have to go," said Beverly. She couldn't stand it — any of it — Jerome's cruelty, Elmer's trembling hands.

Elmer shook his head. He looked down at his hands, and then he looked up — away from her, past her. "Sure," he said. "Go."

She left Zoom City and went back to Mr. C's. Jerome's truck was gone.

She wanted to destroy something.

She wanted to sit down in the empty parking lot and cry.

Instead, she went down to the beach. She stood and stared at the big indifferent ocean. It sparkled as if nothing at all were wrong. The sand was hot. The sky was a merciless blue — not a lapis lazuli blue, not an angel-wing blue, but the washed-out, giving-up blue of the end of things, the blue of August in Florida.

Who would put duct tape over someone's

mouth? Who would duct-tape someone to a chair and lock them in a closet?

Jerome.

That was who.

It was terrible.

Everything was terrible.

Twenty-three

Beverly sat down in the hot sand.

She took the picture of happy Mr. Denby out of her pocket. Happy Mr. Denby and his happy wife and his happy kids. She looked at the snow falling outside the window. She stared at the bare branches of the tree. She studied the face of the toothless, smiling kid.

Photographs like this were a lie.

They promised something impossible.

People were terrible to other people. That was the truth.

She wanted Buddy.

She wished he were sitting next to her, leaning into her, his flank rising and falling. Buddy, who was always gentle. Buddy, who had never hurt anybody.

But Buddy was gone from the world and Jerome was in it.

There was no equity in that—none at all.

The ocean kept pounding in, ferocious, relentless. Beverly rested her chin on her knees.

A kid with a sand bucket came and stood too close to her. "What are you looking at?" he said.

"None of your business," she told him. She put the photo back in her pocket.

"Move," said the boy.

"What? No."

"I'm going to build a sandcastle here."

"Build it somewhere else," said Beverly.

The kid was maybe six or seven years old. He stared at Beverly, and she stared back. "I'm going to tell my mom," he said.

"Good," she said. "I don't care."

The boy blinked. There was sand in his eyebrows and his eyelashes. His shoulders were sunburned.

"There she is, right over there." He pointed at a woman sitting on a towel. The woman waved. "She can get really, really mad."

"Yeah, well, I'm not afraid of her," said Beverly.

"You're not?"

"No," said Beverly.

"I am," said the boy. He sighed. "When she gets really mad—then I'm afraid of her." He rubbed at his eyebrows. "But I can't talk anymore. I have to build this castle." He sighed again. He pointed at a spot to the left of Beverly. "And I have to build it right there."

"Look," said Beverly. "Do you want me to help you out?"

"Yes," he said. "Obviously, that's what I want."

They worked together in silence for a long time. The boy went down to the water and got wet sand and brought it back up, bucket after bucket. Beverly shaped the sand into towers and arches. She dug a moat.

"You're good at making castles," said the boy.

"Yeah," said Beverly. "I know."

Later he said, "You smell like ketchup."

"You don't smell so great yourself," said Beverly.

The boy laughed.

The mother came over when they were halfway done and said, "Robbie, we have to go now."

"I'm busy," he said.

"You can come back tomorrow," said his mother.

"Everything will be gone tomorrow," said Robbie.

"Everything will be right here," said his mother.

"She'll be gone," he said, pointing at Beverly.

"I'll come back," said Beverly.

Robbie studied her.

"Okay," he said finally. And he let his mother take his hand.

"Thanks," the woman said to Beverly.

Beverly shrugged. "Sure," she said.

"I'll meet you here tomorrow," said Robbie. "Right here." He pointed at the sandcastle.

"Okay," said Beverly.

She sat by the half-finished castle for a few

minutes after Robbie left. She thought about how everyone lied to little kids without even thinking that they were lying.

Everything will be right here.

I'll come back.

Right.

There were so many stupid things in the world that it was hard to keep track of them all. She thought about Elmer—his face gone white, his hands shaking. She thought about Jerome and his beefy, sneering self.

And then for some reason, she thought about Nod's tail hanging down from the top of the refrigerator, ticking back and forth, back and forth. She thought about the angel—how she hung there in the sky, waiting, her blue wings lit up with lapis lazuli. She thought about Iola putting a tuna melt down on the table in the little kitchen.

In a crooked little house.

By a crooked little sea.

Beverly got up. She walked over the hot sand, up to A1A, and back to the Seahorse Court.

Twenty-four

Iola was sitting out in front of the trailer. Nod was in her lap.

"I've been waiting for you, darling," said Iola. She smiled. "Don't tell me not to wait, because I'm waiting. And look at this!" She waved a piece of paper over her head, and then held it out to Beverly.

Beverly took the paper. "Christmas in July at the VFW," she read. "Win the world's largest turkey! Dance to a live band! Trim the tree! Refreshments: Cheese! Crackers! Punch! Good times for one and all. From five p.m. until the cows come home."

There was a picture of a turkey down at the bottom of the page. He was smiling, which was stupid, since somebody was going to cook him and eat him. There were Christmas lights around the border of the page and a grinning Santa up in the right-hand corner. Next to Santa's head was the word Ho.

Not Ho, ho, ho.

Just Ho.

"It's August," said Beverly, handing the flyer back to Iola. "How can they have Christmas in July in August?"

"They have Christmas in July every year, and I suppose they didn't get everything put together in time this year. I thought maybe they wasn't going to have it at all. But now, here they are having it, and it is tomorrow night! Can you believe it? I'm just so excited. It's for all ages—you can go, too. Oh, it is a good time. It is just so much fun. I love to dance. Don't you love to dance?"

"No," said Beverly.

"Everybody loves to dance," said Iola. "And this year, they are having a contest for the world's largest turkey. They have had turkey giveaways before, but they've never had one where you could win the world's largest turkey."

"Can Elmer come over here for dinner?" said Beverly.

"Who?" said Iola.

"Elmer. My friend. The friend I made yesterday."

"Elmer, your friend. Of course he can. When?"

"Today? Tonight? Now?"

"Yes," said Iola. "Yes." She smiled up at Beverly. Her wig was crooked. Her eyes were huge behind her glasses.

"I'll just go and invite him, then," said Beverly.

"Well, my goodness," said Iola. "I guess I will get up out of this chair and start cooking. Tuna melts?"

"Tuna melts," said Beverly.

She walked up to A1A. She walked past Mr. C's, past the phone booth. She went up to Zoom City. She walked past the metal horse with his front legs stretched out as if he were going somewhere, when really he wasn't going anywhere at all.

Elmer looked up when she walked in, and then he looked away.

"Do you like tuna melts?" she said.

Elmer didn't say anything.

"Can you come over for dinner tonight?"

Elmer was silent.

"Okay," said Beverly. "How about this one? What's the square root of two?"

"When are you going to stop asking me questions?" said Elmer.

"I don't know," said Beverly. "Maybe when you start answering some. So. Can you come over for dinner tonight?"

He turned his head and looked at her. "No," he said.

"Why not?"

"Don't pity me," he said.

"I don't pity you."

"Yeah? Well, did Jerome tell you what he used to call me?"

"Fudd," said Beverly.

"Right, Fudd."

"So what?" said Beverly.

"So th-th-that's all, folks. I don't need your pity.

I don't need to come to your house and eat tuna melts."

"It's not my house," said Beverly. "It's just where I'm staying. It's a trailer, a pink trailer. It belongs to an old lady named Iola. She has a cat named Nod."

Elmer shook his head.

"It's close to the ocean," said Beverly. "So it's a crooked little trailer by a crooked little sea."

Elmer smiled. He looked down at his hands.

"Come on," said Beverly.

The door to Zoom City opened, and a man with a beard walked in. He was in his bare feet. He nodded to Elmer, and Elmer nodded back. The man walked over to the cooler.

From where she was standing, Beverly could see the horse outside—bolted into place, waiting.

"I don't think so," said Elmer.

"In a crooked little house by a crooked little sea," said Beverly. "You wrote those words, didn't you?"

"No," he said. He shook his head. He looked up at her. "No, I told you I didn't. Why do you keep thinking it was me?"

"Because I like the words so much," she said. "Because they make sense to me."

He smiled again.

"I'll wait here," she said. "It's almost five. I'll just wait outside for you. And then after dinner, I'll drive you home. Iola has a Pontiac."

"Gee!" said Elmer. "A Pontiac! And no, thank you. You're not old enough to drive me anywhere."

"I'm a great driver," said Beverly. "I'll wait for you outside. Okay?"

"Do whatever you want to do," said Elmer.

Twenty-five

Beverly was walking out of Zoom City when Mrs. Deely materialized out of nowhere and grabbed hold of her arm.

"I have good news for you," said Mrs. Deely.

"Great," said Beverly.

"I've produced a new installment, and I would like to share it with you." Mrs. Deely was wearing the same duck-covered skirt she had on the day before, but today, there were three pencils shoved in the mountain of her hair, instead of just one.

"I've been called to draw the truth," said Mrs. Deely.

"Yeah," said Beverly. "You told me."

Mrs. Deely handed Beverly a piece of paper. Beverly looked down at it and saw more snakes. And some lightning. And a lot of stick people dancing in the middle of a fire.

"Go on, take it," said Mrs. Deely. "It's for you. I must continue on. There are more people, young people, in need of the truth. It's best to learn the truth when you are young."

Mrs. Deely walked toward a kid who had just climbed on the horse.

"Hallllloooooo," Mrs. Deely called.

The kid was maybe four years old. His hair was shaved close to his head, and his mother was standing next to him. His mother said, "Isn't this fun, Johnny? Isn't this the most fun you have ever had?"

Beverly hated it when people told you how much fun you were having.

The horse started moving up and down in a resigned way.

"Isn't it fun, Johnny?" said his mother.

The kid nodded. He didn't seem all that convinced.

"I have the truth for you, Johnny," said Mrs. Deely, walking over to the kid and holding out a paper.

Johnny looked at Mrs. Deely.

"Who are you?" said Johnny's mother.

"I am the messenger," said Mrs. Deely.

The door to Zoom City opened. Elmer stuck his head out. "Mrs. Deely!" he shouted. "Do not give him that paper!"

"But it's the truth," said Mrs. Deely. "And I am called upon to deliver it. I must deliver it."

"Give it to me," said Beverly.

"But you already have one," said Mrs. Deely.

"I'll give this one to a friend," said Beverly.

"Really?" said Mrs. Deely. She smiled a radiant smile. "Thank you. Please do share it. That would be so wonderful." She put out her hand and patted Johnny on the head.

"Stop that," said the mother.

"Good-bye, Mrs. Deely," said Elmer in a loud voice. "Thank you very much."

He looked at Beverly.

She held herself very still.

"Fine," he said. "You win."

"Great," she said.

"I'll be out in a few minutes."

"I'll be here," said Beverly. She folded up Mrs. Deely's two pieces of paper and shoved them in her back pocket along with Mr. Denby's happy family photo.

And then she stood and watched Johnny ride the horse.

He held on to the plastic reins and stared back at her.

"It's so fun, Johnny," said the mother. "Right?"

Right, thought Beverly.

Elmer came out of Zoom City with his book bag slung over his shoulder. "See what I'm talking about with Mrs. Deely?" he said. "What if the kid could read? It would scare the crap out of him."

"That horse drives me crazy," said Beverly.

"The horse makes kids happy, mostly," said Elmer. "It's Mrs. Deely who drives me crazy."

They walked past the phone booth. It was

glittering—shining in the hot sun. They both looked over at it at the same time.

"In a crooked little house," said Elmer.

"By a crooked little sea," said Beverly. She smiled a gigantic smile.

"What did you do to your tooth?" said Elmer.

"What?" said Beverly.

"Your front tooth is chipped."

Beverly shrugged. "I was a kid."

"And?"

"And I was running away from one of my mother's boyfriends."

Elmer nodded slowly. "Why?"

"Because he was chasing me."

"Uh-huh," said Elmer. "Why was he chasing you?"

"Because I had his wallet," said Beverly.

"Oh," said Elmer. "Right. Of course you did."

The sun was beating down on them.

"I took his wallet, and he figured out that it was me who took it, and he chased me down the street yelling, 'You worthless brat! Give me back my wallet!' He was in his underwear, which made it pretty funny. And I was running as fast as I could, and then I tripped and fell on my face and chipped my tooth. After that, my mother stopped dating him. Or more like he stopped dating my mother. Because I was such a worthless little brat."

"That stinks," said Elmer.

"Right, well. I don't care. I didn't care."

The cars roaring past them sounded like the ocean, or the ocean sounded like the cars. It was hard to tell the difference. A plane flew overhead trailing a banner that said EVERY HOUR IS HAPPY HOUR.

They both looked up.

"I will be so glad to get out of this place," said Elmer.

"Yeah," said Beverly. "Right. New Hampshire."

"New Hampshire," said Elmer.

"To get away from Jerome?"

"No," said Elmer. "There are Jeromes everywhere you go. You can never get away from the Jeromes of the world."

"Why didn't you fight him? Why didn't you fight back?"

Elmer shrugged.

"I would have beat the crap out of him," said Beverly. "I'm thinking about beating the crap out of him right now."

"Not everyone is you," said Elmer. He moved his book bag to his other shoulder. "Not everyone eats glue and steals wallets."

Beverly laughed. "This is it," she said. She pointed at the trailer park sign. "We're at the Seahorse Court."

She led Elmer down the white driveway to the little pink trailer.

Twenty-six

Iola was standing out front. "Howdy, howdy!" she called when she saw them. She walked toward Elmer with her hand out, smiling. "Now," she said, "you are Beverly's friend. You are Elmer."

"Yes, ma'am," said Elmer. He took hold of her hand.

"I'm Iola Jenkins."

"How do you do?" he said.

"I do just fine," said Iola. "My goodness, you're tall. Do you dance?"

"Not really," said Elmer. "I mean I never have. I don't know how."

"How about I teach you?" said Iola. "There's a dance tomorrow night at the VFW. The three of us could go."

"Iola," said Beverly.

"Shhhhh," said Iola. "Let the boy make up his own mind." She pulled the flyer out of her dress pocket and presented it to Elmer. "Ta-da," she said.

"Christmas in July," Elmer read. He looked at Iola. "But it's August."

"You just think about it," said Iola. She patted his arm and took the flyer from him, folded it, and put it back in her pocket. "For now, come on inside, both of you. I made tuna melts. And peas."

They went into the trailer. Beverly and Elmer sat down at the little table. Iola put a sandwich down in front of Elmer. "Thank you," he said.

Iola came back to the table with a tuna melt for Beverly and one for herself. She gave everyone a scoop of peas. "Scooch over, darling," she said to Beverly.

Iola sat down in the chair next to Beverly with

an "oof." She smiled across the table at Elmer. She said, "It's usually just her and me at this table, just the two of us. And before she showed up, it was just me. But now, there's three. Three of us. That's good. I like it when the numbers go up instead of down, don't you?"

"Yes, ma'am," said Elmer.

Nod came walking through the kitchen, his tail held high.

"That's Nod," said Iola.

"Yeah," said Elmer. "I heard about Nod."

"Watch," said Beverly.

Nod leaped up on top of the refrigerator and put his back to them. His tail started twitching. He stared at the wall.

"What's he looking at?" said Elmer.

"He's looking for a door," said Beverly.

"A door to another world," said Elmer.

"Right," said Beverly. She couldn't help it. She smiled at him.

"No, no," said Iola. "There's only this world. Besides, Nod ain't going anywhere just yet."

"How did he get the name Nod?" asked Elmer.

"Because of Wynken, Blynken, and Nod," said Iola, "who sailed off in a wooden shoe."

"'But I shall name you the fishermen three: Wynken, Blynken, and Nod,'" said Elmer.

"Yes," said Iola. "Just like that. Only there aren't three anymore. There used to be a Wynken and a Blynken. Now there's just a Nod. That's how it is when you get old: you watch all the people and all the cats and all the dogs—and oh, just everything and everyone—you watch them all marching on past you, leaving without you."

Yeah, thought Beverly, *I get it.*

Iola looked down at her hands, and then back up again. She said, "And that is why you go to dances every chance you get."

"Will you stop about the dance?" said Beverly.

"I'll go," said Elmer.

"What?" said Beverly.

Elmer shrugged. "I'll go," he said again.

"We'll all go," said Iola. She clapped her hands together. "Goody."

After dinner, they went out onto the porch and played cards. The crickets started up, competing with the sound of the ocean.

Beverly closed her eyes. The EVERY HOUR IS HAPPY HOUR banner flashed through her mind, and she heard Elmer saying that he couldn't wait to leave. And even though the world was loud with living things, she suddenly felt lonely.

She opened her eyes. "Elmer's leaving," she said to Iola. "He's going to Dartmouth."

"Is that right?" said Iola. "Now, where is that?"

"New Hampshire," said Elmer.

"He's going to be an engineer," said Beverly. "But he really likes art."

Elmer shrugged. "I like to look at art. And I like to draw." His face got red. "I'm not that good at it, but I like it."

"Well, why don't you paint me?" said Iola. She put down her cards. "I have always wanted someone to paint my picture."

"I can't really paint," said Elmer. "I just draw—with a pencil, a charcoal pencil."

"I know what," said Iola. "You should draw a

picture of me from when I wasn't old. That's what you should do. Wait right here." She got up and left the porch and came back a minute later holding a silver frame with a black-and-white picture in it.

"That's me," she said, pointing at a tiny smiling woman. "On my wedding day. And that's Tommy, my husband. That's me," she said again. "Can you believe it?"

Beverly looked at the young Iola smiling out of the photograph.

"You were beautiful," she said.

"Pshaw," said Iola. "I was happy is all. I loved Tommy, and he loved me. You know how I met him? We was in a play together. I was six years old, and he was seven. He was the sun, and I was the moon. Can you believe it? The sun and the moon. They raised us up high on ropes, way up above the stage. First the sun went up, and then it came down. That was Tommy. And then the moon rose up, and that was me. First came the sun, and then came the moon. I still remember my line: 'Oh, world, I cast my dappled light upon you.'"

"What was Tommy's line?" said Elmer.

"'I shine the livelong day. I shine strong and brave and true,'" said Iola. "And that was the truth. He did. He was a good man. And a good dancer! Oh, he could dance. Everyone danced then."

"Do you want me to draw you?" said Elmer. "I could do it right now."

"You could?" said Iola. "Me now? Or me then?"

"Both," said Elmer, "if you want."

He got up off the couch and went and got his book bag. He pulled out a sketch pad and a pencil. "Sit next to the lamp," he said to Iola. "And hold yourself as still as you can."

Nod came in from the kitchen, hopped into Beverly's lap, and curled himself into a tight ball.

"Stupid cat," said Beverly. She ran her hand over him—his small head and his bony back. Nod started to purr.

Elmer looked up at Iola, and then down at the paper, and then back up at Iola again. Moths flitted against the louvers of the porch, trying to get inside, closer to the light.

"I could draw you, too," said Elmer, without looking at Beverly. "If you wanted."

Nod purred louder.

"I don't need anybody to draw me," said Beverly.

"Oh, honey," said Iola. "Don't say that. It would be wonderful to have a picture of you."

Elmer looked up from the sketch pad. He glanced at Beverly, and then he looked away.

He was smiling.

Twenty-seven

Beverly and Elmer walked down to the beach afterward.

They sat in the sand. Elmer sat close to her, his arm brushing up against hers.

"That made her happy," said Beverly.

"Yeah, well," said Elmer. "It's not that great a drawing."

"No," said Beverly, "I mean all of it. Us being there."

"Us?" said Elmer. He lay back. He put his arms behind his head.

"Us," said Beverly. "You and me. Elmer and Beverly. Beverly and Elmer. However you want to say it."

"The sun and the moon?"

"Right," said Beverly. "Sure."

She lay back in the sand, too.

There were stars in the sky — not a lot of them, but enough to convince you that there was something bright somewhere behind all of that darkness. And there was a moon, or a part of a moon, shining dimly.

"I have this friend who disappeared," Beverly said, not sure why she was even saying it. "Her name is Louisiana Elefante, and she lived with her granny, and a few years ago, she and her granny just disappeared."

"Disappeared?" said Elmer.

"Disappeared. Just gone, you know? We went looking for her. Me and this other friend, Raymie."

For some reason, it felt strange to say Raymie's name out loud.

She said it again. "Raymie."

"Raymie," repeated Elmer.

"Yeah, Raymie. She's my best friend. Anyway, we went to the house where Louisiana and her grandmother lived, and it was empty. You could hear your voice echo. I mean, it was always empty—they didn't have any furniture. But this was a different kind of empty. You could tell just by the way the house felt that they were gone, you know? It was terrible, walking through the house, looking and not finding anybody. I'll never forget that feeling."

"What happened to her?"

"She's in Georgia now," said Beverly. "She found a family."

Elmer didn't say anything. She could hear him breathing. Even with the crash and mutter of waves, she could hear Elmer's breath.

"What about your family?" he said.

"I used to have a dog. Buddy. He was from the pound. Me and Louisiana and Raymie rescued him. Anyway, Buddy died. And I buried him in the backyard, and then I came here because I couldn't stand it—that empty feeling."

"What about your mother?" said Elmer.

"What about her?"

"Does she know where you are?"

"I called her. I told her I'm okay."

"Are you going back?" said Elmer.

"I don't know," said Beverly.

"My parents are really glad that I got this scholarship to Dartmouth," said Elmer, "and they're really glad that I get to go away to school. But my mother cries about it all the time, too."

"Because you're leaving?"

"Uh-huh," said Elmer. "I'm her baby."

"Yeah. Well, I'm not my mother's baby. And she's fine without me. She's drunk most of the time anyway. She doesn't know if I'm coming or going."

"I bet she pays more attention to you than you think," said Elmer.

"I doubt it," said Beverly. "At work, there's this woman named Doris. She's the cook. She keeps an eye on me. She's always giving Freddie—the waitress—the business, making sure that Freddie tips out with me. Doris keeps talking about equity. Equity is her favorite word. I was thinking about that — how no matter what, things are never fair."

Elmer turned his head and looked at her. "Yeah," he said. "But I guess you have to keep working to try and make them fair, don't you? Otherwise, what's the point in being here?" He turned his head back and looked up at the sky. "I can see stars," he said.

"I know," said Beverly. "I can see them, too."

"'The little stars were the herring fish that lived in the beautiful sea,'" said Elmer.

"What?"

"That's part of 'Wynken, Blynken, and Nod'— that poem. The nursery rhyme."

"What's the rest of it?"

"'Now cast your nets wherever you wish — never afraid are we!' And '"Where are you going and what do you wish?" the old moon asked the three.' I just know bits and pieces. I don't know the whole thing."

"When Buddy died, when we buried him, we said some poetry. Raymie said we had to. It was that one about slipping the surly bonds. Do you know that one?"

"Yeah," said Elmer. "I know that one. I like that

poem. I like poetry. I don't write it, but I like it a lot. That's something you're not supposed to say out loud if you're a guy. In case someone like Jerome hears you. And then beats the crap out of you, for being a poetry-loving sissy." He sat up suddenly. He shouted, "I like poetry!"

He turned to her. He was smiling. She could see his teeth, white in the darkness. "That felt good," he said. "You should try it. Shout the truth about something."

Beverly sat up. She wasn't going to shout that she loved poetry, because she wasn't certain that she did. What was the truth? The truth was that she missed Buddy. She missed Raymie. She missed Louisiana.

"I miss everyone!"

That's what she ended up shouting.

And then, "I miss my father!"

It felt strange to say it, shout it, admit it.

"Where is he?" said Elmer. "Your dad?"

"Gone," said Beverly. "I don't know. New York. At least that's where he was last time I knew anything about it. He slipped the surly bonds."

"Right," said Elmer. He lay back down. "Those good old surly bonds. Do you know what the janitor said to me?"

"What janitor?"

"Mr. Jerowski. The guy who yelled at me in Polish when he found me tied up in his closet. After he was done yelling, he took all the duct tape off, and his hands were shaking. He was crying. He kept saying, 'Fast, fast. I do it fast. It hurts less fast.'

"I wanted to tell him that it was okay, that I was fine. But I couldn't make myself say it. And he kept crying and saying, 'I'm sorry to hurt you. I'm sorry to hurt you.' Like that, over and over." Elmer shook his head. "He cried. And I cried."

Beverly reached over and grabbed Elmer's hand. She didn't hold on to it. She just squeezed it and then let it go.

"How does it go with the herrings again?" she said.

"'The little stars were the herring fish that lived in the beautiful sea.'"

"Yeah," said Beverly. "That is incredibly, incredibly stupid—fish being stars."

"Most everything is incredibly stupid," said Elmer. "Speaking of which: Wanna go to a dance?"

"Sure," said Beverly. "We could maybe win the world's largest turkey."

"We could," said Elmer.

Beverly sat with her arms wrapped around her knees and looked up at the stars—or the herring fish, or whatever they were—shining up there.

"And the part about the nets?" she said. "How does that go?"

But Elmer didn't answer her. She looked over at him. He was asleep.

"It was like, cast your nets wherever you want," she said. "Right? Don't be afraid to cast your nets, and you will maybe catch yourself some herring fish that twinkle like stars."

She lay down next to him.

She listened to the ocean, to Elmer breathing.

The sand was still warm.

Twenty-eight

When Beverly got to Mr. C's the next day, the door had a sign on it that said:

Unfortunately, we are experiencing some small problems and will be closed today. Please visit us tomorrow for the best fish in the C!

Sincerely, Mr. C

Beverly tried the door. It was locked. She went around back. The kitchen door was propped open with the cement block, and Charles and Doris were in the kitchen, sitting on tall stools at a metal table.

They were playing cards. The little fan from Mr. Denby's office was on the floor, turning and turning, still searching for something.

"Hey," said Beverly.

"Hey yourself, Aunt Beverly," said Doris.

Charles nodded at her. His green knit cap was pulled down low over his eyes.

"What's going on?" said Beverly.

"It's a strike," said Doris.

"What?"

"We're on strike," said Doris.

"What's that mean?"

"You know exactly what it means," said Doris. "Some justice. Some equity. Benefits for one thing. Better pay for another. It means I'm not cooking and Charles is not washing dishes until things change."

"Things need to change," said Charles.

"Right," said Doris. "And how do things change?"

"You make them change," said Charles.

"That's right," said Doris.

"Where's Mr. Denby?" said Beverly.

"He's in his office, I'm sure — sitting at his desk

with his head in his hands. He's in there thinking, *How am I going to get out of this?* But guess what? It's too late. He can't get out of it."

Doris slammed both her hands down on the metal table, and Beverly felt a small jolt go through her.

"It's time to make things change," said Doris.

Freddie came into the kitchen. She put her hands on her hips and said, "You people are ruining everything for everyone else."

"So you say," said Doris. She shuffled the cards.

"It's not right," said Freddie.

"You play cards?" Doris said to Beverly.

"Sure," said Beverly.

"Pull up a stool, then."

"Don't do it," said Freddie. "You could be a waitress. You could be a model. You could be a Living Darlene."

"I don't want to be a Living Darlene," said Beverly.

"What's a living Darlene?" said Charles.

"Somebody famous," said Freddie.

"Fame ain't all it's cracked up to be, if you ask

me," said Charles. He adjusted his knit cap.

"I wasn't asking you," said Freddie. "And what do you know about it, anyway? You were nothing but a football player. Big deal and so what."

Doris started to deal the cards.

Freddie said, "This is ridiculous."

Mr. Denby came into the kitchen. His mustache looked crooked. His hair was standing up on top of his head. "Are we ready to move along now?" he said. "Are we ready to cook some fish?"

"No," said Doris. "We aren't."

Mr. Denby put both his hands on top of his head and pushed down hard. It was as if he were working to keep his head attached to his shoulders. "I am raising three children," he said.

"Yep," said Doris. She slapped a card down on the table. "I've raised five children. I've got sixteen grandchildren."

"What are we playing?" said Beverly.

"Poker," said Doris.

"I'm working to make the world better for my kids," said Mr. Denby.

"That's the thing," said Doris. "That's it right

there. You need to be working to make it better for all of us. I want sick days. I want some insurance. I'm tired of getting paid under the table."

"I want the world to be a better place for all of us, too," said Freddie.

Doris snorted.

Mr. Denby walked around the kitchen, alternately pulling at his hair and pushing his head down on his shoulders. He looked into the fish fryer.

"Do you know how to work this?" he said.

"I sure do," said Doris.

"I'm not talking to you," said Mr. Denby.

"Good," said Doris. "I'm not talking to you, either."

"Mr. Denby?" said Freddie. "If I don't wait tables, I don't get any money. Are you going to pay us for being here today?"

"Pay you?" said Mr. Denby. "Pay you for what? You're not working. I've got three children I need to support. My wife isn't talking to me. I can't explain why — it's too complicated to explain. Sometimes, things happen that you just can't explain to other people. Or to yourself for that matter. And you surely can't explain it to your children. Just try explaining things to children! What I'm saying is that sometimes things spin out of control." Mr. Denby put both his hands on his head and pushed down.

"Yep," said Doris.

Beverly thought about the photo of Mr. Denby at Christmas. She knew it was a lie. All those Santa hats and those smiles — all that happiness.

"Mr. Denby," said Freddie, "I'm trying to save my money so that I can move to Hollywood and live out my destiny. If you're not going to pay me, then I need to find another job."

"Fine," said Mr. Denby. He had taken his hands off the top of his head and was fiddling with one of the knobs on the giant stove.

"But, Mr. Denby, I'm your best waitress."

"You're the only waitress," said Doris. "And, Mr. Denby, you should leave those knobs alone. You don't know what you're doing, and there's no point in you blowing us all to kingdom come. Now, I'm no fool. I know that this restaurant makes good money. I want you to go back to your office and get out your adding machine and figure out how you can pay us all some kind of living wage, along with some kind of benefits. Do the paperwork."

"Right," said Mr. Denby. "Okay."

He bent down and unplugged the fan.

"Do not," said Doris, "take that fan."

"Right," said Mr. Denby. He plugged the fan back in. He stood up. He put his hands on his head and walked out of the kitchen.

"This is terrible," said Freddie. "This is the worst thing that's ever happened to me."

Charles shook his head. "This?" he said. "This is nothing."

Beverly pulled a stool up to the table. She picked up her cards.

"You can't stay with them," Freddie said to Beverly.

"Yes, I can," said Beverly.

"Well, I'm not staying," said Freddie.

"Good," said Charles.

"Good," said Doris.

"Good," said Beverly.

Freddie left, and the seagull appeared at the

open back door. He studied the three of them with beady eyes.

Doris said, "You understand that Charles and I aren't going anywhere, right? We're not going to leave this kitchen until Mr. Denby gives in. We'll stay here all day and night if we have to."

"You're going to stay overnight?" said Beverly.

"Whatever it takes," said Doris. "After all, we've got plenty of food. Lots of fish."

Freddie came flouncing back into the kitchen. "You should stop this," she said. "It's not going to work. He'll just find somebody else to cook fish. He'll just find somebody else to do the dishes. You can be replaced."

"I'm not moving," said Doris.

"You should get up," Freddie said to Beverly. "Things aren't going to change. You're on the wrong side."

"No," said Beverly.

Freddie left the kitchen again.

"She'll be back," said Charles. "That's how it is with people like her."

Doris sighed. "Don't I know it," she said.

The seagull turned his head from left to right, considering. He hopped closer to the threshold.

"No," said Doris without even looking in the seagull's direction. She pounded her fist on the metal table. "No, you do not."

The seagull hopped backward.

"We are playing five-card draw," said Doris.

"Okay," said Beverly.

Five minutes later, Freddie came back into the kitchen. "We're in charge of our own destinies, you know."

"Yep," said Doris.

"Okay, well, I'm not talking to you, Doris. I'm talking to Beverly. I can't believe what a traitor you are. I'm the reason you got hired in the first place. Plus I made that name tag for you."

Beverly shrugged. "You spelled my name wrong," she said. "And I'm not doing anything. I'm just sitting here playing poker."

"Traitor," said Freddie. And she turned and left again.

Beverly stared at her cards. She studied the haughty, disdainful face on the queen of diamonds.

It reminded her of the face of the angel in the painting.

Outside the open door, past the seagull and the dumpsters and the hotels, there was a small strip of ocean visible. It was a bright, sparkling blue.

Not as bright as lapis lazuli.

But bright enough.

Beverly suddenly felt as if she were exactly where she was supposed to be.

Doris knocked on the table. "It's your turn, Aunt Beverly," she said. "Don't stop paying attention now."

Twenty-nine

Beverly stayed at Mr. C's for most of the afternoon and then went down to Zoom City to meet Elmer.

"I guess I don't have a job anymore," she said. "I kind of feel like I should be in the kitchen with Doris and Charles, you know? Like maybe I should have stayed there with them—on strike. But I need to get Iola to the dance. I promised I would."

They were on the side of A1A, walking to Iola's. Elmer had a suit jacket slung over his shoulder.

"What you should do is go home," said Elmer.

"Yeah," said Beverly. "Duh. That's where we're going."

"No," said Elmer. "I mean your real home. I mean you should go back."

"I don't want to go back."

"What about school?"

"What about it?

"It's starting soon. You need to stay in school. You need to graduate."

"So I can go to college?" said Beverly. "On a full scholarship? To Dartmouth?"

Elmer shrugged. "It could happen."

"No. It couldn't."

"All kinds of things happen that you don't think could ever happen," Elmer said.

"Right," said Beverly. "Sure they do."

Iola was waiting for them out front. She was dressed for the dance. She was wearing a flowered dress and green shoes. She had on rouge.

Elmer said, "You look great, Mrs. Jenkins."

"You brought a jacket," said Iola.

"Yeah, and look what else I brought." He pulled a striped tie out of his book bag.

"You brought a tie!" said Iola.

"It's a dance, right? I've got to dress right."

He reached back into his book bag and took out a piece of paper. He held the paper out to Beverly. "This is for you," he said.

"What is it?"

"It's a picture. Of you," he said. "Duh."

Beverly looked down at the face on the paper. She didn't recognize it. She knew that it was her, but at the same time, it didn't make any sense that it was her.

"Will you look at that?" said Iola. "You're so beautiful."

"Thanks," Beverly said to Elmer. She looked up at him, and then she looked back down again. She felt mad for some reason that she didn't understand. She folded the paper in half.

"Honey!" said Iola. "What are you doing? Don't do that. You'll ruin it."

"It's fine," said Elmer. His face was very red. "I don't care."

"Give it to me," said Iola.

Beverly handed the paper to Iola, who worked to straighten out the crease. Her hands were shaking.

"It doesn't matter," said Elmer.

"Yes, it does," said Iola.

"Let's just go," said Beverly. "It starts at five, right? Let's just go to the stupid dance."

Beverly drove the Pontiac.

Iola sat in the front, and Elmer sat in the back with his jacket on and his arms crossed over his striped tie.

"Oh, I'm just so excited," said Iola. "My heart is beating so fast. I hope I win the turkey."

Beverly looked at Elmer in the rearview mirror. She raised her eyebrows at him and smiled. But he didn't smile back.

When they got to the VFW, Iola went right through the door, straight inside, without even looking back at them. "Hurry up, you two," she called over her shoulder.

"I'm sorry that I bent it," Beverly said to Elmer. "The picture, I mean."

"It's fine," said Elmer. "I don't care."

"It scared me. I don't know. It's like I looked at it, and I recognized myself and I also didn't recognize myself."

Elmer shook his head.

"I'm sorry," she said again.

She looked up at him. But he was looking away from her, staring up at the VFW sign.

"There's a bird's nest right there," she said, pointing to the V.

"Yeah," he said. "I see it."

His face was in profile to her. The skin on it looked tight and painful.

"Does it hurt?" she said.

"Does what hurt?"

"Your face."

"Yeah," he said. "I know this one. I'm supposed to say, 'No, why?' And then you say, 'Because it's sure killing me.'"

"It's not killing me," said Beverly. "It's doing the opposite of killing me."

Elmer was quiet for a minute, staring up at the sign, and then he nodded. "Yes," he said. "It hurts. But so what? Lots of things hurt. It won't last forever. Someday, it will clear up. That's what my mother says. No one has acne on their face for their whole life, right?"

Just then the sign sputtered to life. The V and the F and the W were suddenly lit and glowing. Beverly looked up at the letters and thought about the angel again, about how she had come to deliver important news.

Annunciation.

That's what Elmer had said the painting was called.

Annunciation.

The angel had come to make an announcement to Mary.

And you knew something important was happening in the painting because the angel had wings like blue fire.

But in real life, how did you know who was announcing what?

Maybe the VFW sign was announcing something. Maybe Mrs. Deely and her cartoons were annunciations. Maybe the mechanical horse was trying to deliver a message. And surely Doris had come to announce something.

Maybe everything and everyone in the world should be painted with blue wings.

"Where do you get lapis lazuli?" Beverly asked Elmer.

"I don't know," he said. "I'm not sure. Somewhere far away—the Middle East, maybe? I'll find out where."

She took hold of his hand and squeezed it.

And then she tried to let go of him, but he wouldn't let her.

"No," he said.

"Beverly and Elmer!" Iola called. She was standing at the door to the VFW. She waved to them. "Come on inside and dance."

"I can tell you one thing," said Beverly. "I'm not dancing."

"Let's go," said Elmer.

Beverly walked inside with him, still holding his hand.

Thirty

Inside the VFW, it was dark and twinkly lights were strung everywhere. There was a stage with a Christmas tree on it.

The floors were wood, and they creaked when you stepped on them. The whole place was noisy with people talking and laughing. Music was playing, and a man dressed up in a Santa Claus suit was walking through the crowd shouting, "Ho, ho, ho! Merry Christmas!"

At a card table off to one side, there was a blue ceramic bowl full of tickets. And next to the card table, there was a very long table covered in butcher paper. There was a punch bowl on the long table, and a tower of Styrofoam cups and a big platter of cheese cubes with a little frilled toothpick stuck in each piece of cheese. Next to the food table, there was another card table with a record player on it. Someone on the record was singing "Have Yourself a Merry Little Christmas."

A cloud of cigarette smoke hung over the room. The smoke made the lights and the Christmas tree and the people all seem unreal. It was like looking at someone else's dream.

Iola said, "Who wants some punch?"

"I'll get it," said Elmer.

"Oh, there is Frederick Morton," said Iola to Beverly. "I haven't seen him since the last dance. I'll be right back."

"Turkey tickets," said a little man in a blue cap holding a fistful of red flowers and a roll of tickets. "Win the world's largest turkey. I also got poppies for sale."

"How much are the turkey tickets?" said Beverly.

"Fifty cents," he said. "Fifty cents to win the world's largest turkey. I'll throw in a poppy with each ticket." The man didn't have any teeth. He smiled at her, displaying his gums.

"I don't want a poppy," said Beverly. She handed the man a dollar. "Two tickets."

"What you want to do is write your name on the back of each ticket," he said, "and then drop them over there in that bowl, and you could win yourself the world's largest turkey."

"Got it," said Beverly.

"You ever heard of the trenches?"

"What?" said Beverly.

"The trenches," said the man, "that's where I was. In the trenches. You don't never forget it."

Elmer came over and handed Beverly a cup of punch. She looked down into the cup and saw something floating at the bottom.

"It's a maraschino cherry," said Elmer.

"Right," said Beverly.

"You know about the trenches?" the little man asked Elmer.

"Yes, sir. I've read about the trenches."

"Sure you have. Gonna buy a poppy?"

"Okay," said Elmer. He handed the man a dollar and took a poppy and pinned it to his jacket. He said, "'In Flanders fields, the poppies blow,' right?"

"Don't bother reciting that crap to me," the old man said. "I am ninety-two years old. Ninety-two! I don't never want to hear that stupid poem again. I lived through it." He pounded his fist on his chest. "I lived through that war. I was in them trenches. Nothing describes it. Nothing touches it." He shook his head. "And now, here I am in Tamaray Beach, Florida, selling tickets for the world's largest turkey. Ha-ha-ha. See? That's how life jokes with you. There ain't no sense to it. No sense at all." He smiled, displaying his pink gums again.

"I'll take two tickets," said Elmer.

"That's a dollar. Like I told your girlfriend, you got to write your name on the back of each ticket."

"Thank you," said Elmer.

"You know what I learned after being here on this earth for ninety-two years?"

"No, sir," said Elmer.

The little man leaned in close to them. He whispered, "I ain't learned a thing. Not one thing. Except that there ain't nothing in this world that *can't* happen. That's it. That's the whole of it."

And then he turned away from them and shouted, "Turkey tickets! Get your tickets for the world's largest turkey!"

Beverly finished her punch and went up to the card table. There was a woman sitting behind it knitting a tiny pink sweater.

"Can I borrow something to write with?" said Beverly.

The woman handed her a pen, and Beverly wrote "Iola Jenkins" on the back of each ticket. She dropped the tickets in the blue bowl.

"Thank you, sweetheart," said the woman. "Good luck to you."

And then Iola was behind Beverly, clapping her hands and saying, "The band is here! The band is here! Now the dancing can start."

"Oh, boy," said Beverly.

The band started with "Chattanooga Choo Choo."

Elmer stood beside Beverly. They watched Iola dance with a man wearing a checked jacket. His hair was dyed black.

And then a song called "Moon River" started, and Iola came and took Elmer by the hand and said, "We can waltz to this one, honey."

"I don't know how to waltz," said Elmer.

"A waltz is easy to learn."

"Okay," said Elmer. He put down his punch cup and went off with Iola.

The ninety-two-year-old turkey-ticket man came up to Beverly and smiled at her with his gums.

"Guess how old I am," he said.

"I know how old you are," she said. "Give me twenty dollars' worth of tickets."

"Twenty?" he said.

"No," said Beverly. "Actually, I want forty dollars' worth."

"You want forty dollars' worth?" he said. "The turkey ain't that big."

He counted out the tickets slowly and handed them to Beverly. She went back to the little table.

The knitting woman said, "Well, look who's back!"

"Yeah," said Beverly. "It's me. Can I borrow that pen again?"

"Certainly," said the woman.

Beverly took the pen and got busy writing Iola's name eighty more times.

Elmer was still out on the dance floor in Iola's arms. The room smelled like cigarette smoke and perfume and the ocean, because everything smelled like the ocean in Tamaray Beach.

Beverly realized she was happy, as happy as she had ever been in her life.

It didn't make any sense.

It was stupid.

But she was happy.

She wished that Raymie were at the VFW.

And Louisiana. Louisiana loved a party.

Beverly looked up and out the narrow window that was above the knitting woman's head. She almost expected to see bare branches, snow falling.

Instead, what she saw was the lit-up letter *V* and the flutter of wings.

Her heart skipped a beat.

It was the bird returning home—bringing something back to the nest.

Thirty-one

She wrote Iola's name so many times that her hand started to cramp up.

Iola Jenkins. Iola Jenkins.

Iola Jenkins.

One time in third grade, Beverly had punched Tinsley Amos in the nose. Tinsley was the kind of girl who did everything right, and who was always helpfully pointing out how everybody else did things wrong. Her hair was a shiny gold.

It felt good to punch her.

There was a lot of blood, and Beverly refused to apologize, so she had to stay after school and write sentences on Mrs. Fenstep's blackboard.

I regret my actions.

That was the sentence she wrote. But even after writing the words two hundred times, she didn't regret her actions.

"I hope that you're properly sorry," Mrs. Fenstep said when Beverly was done.

"Not really," said Beverly.

Which meant that she had to write *I am properly sorry* five hundred times on the chalkboard.

Writing Iola's name eighty times was easy in comparison.

It was nothing.

She was happy to write Iola's name.

Underneath the sound of the band playing, there was another kind of music—faint and far away. It sounded like angels singing. Beverly stopped writing for a minute.

She held very still, and then she realized that

it was the record player, still spinning. Some choir was singing "Angels We Have Heard on High."

The happiness inside of Beverly got bigger, wider.

And just after she finished writing Iola's name on the last ticket, Iola appeared beside her, her chest rising and falling. Her face was red. She said, "It's time to dance, honey."

"No," said Beverly. "It's not."

"I taught Elmer, and now he can teach you."

"No," said Beverly.

"Yes, honey," said Iola. "You won't regret it. I promise you."

Beverly stood up.

And then Elmer was there, too.

"There you are," Iola said to him. "Here she is. Here is your Beverly."

"I'm not his Beverly," said Beverly. "And I don't want to dance."

"I can talk you through it," said Elmer. "It's not hard. It's mostly just counting. You can count, right?"

"Ha-ha," said Beverly.

Elmer put his left arm around her waist. "Is that okay?" he said.

"Of course it's okay," said Iola. "You can't dance without touching each other. Teach her the box step. That's the best place to start."

Elmer moved Beverly off, away from Iola. "Okay," he said. "What you should do is imagine a box. We're going to make a box together, with our feet. Look at my feet. Watch."

He moved his feet. He counted to four. "Four sides to a box," he said. "So you count to four."

He made the square again. He counted out loud as he did it. The floor creaked under his feet. The air was heavy with smoke.

"You do it," he said.

Beverly looked down at her feet. She made a square. She didn't bother counting.

"Okay," he said. "Now we're going to do it together. Follow me." He pulled her closer. He started counting in her ear. "One, two, three, four. One, two, three, four."

She followed him.

"Good," he said. "Good."

She looked up at his face, and then past it, out the window of the VFW. She could see the moon.

"The moon is out there," she told him.

"I know it," he said. "I saw it. *Oh, world, I cast my dappled light upon you.* Right?"

Suddenly, Beverly thought she might cry. She bent her head, and Elmer pulled her closer. His shirt smelled like soap and sweat. She could feel his heart beating.

"That's it," said Elmer. "You're doing great. One, two, three, four."

She leaned her head against his chest. She listened to his heart.

"You don't need to keep counting," she said. "I've got it. I understand."

Elmer kept counting anyway.

Thirty-two

And I am pleased to announce that Iola Jenkins has won the world's largest turkey. Iola, are you here tonight?" said the man in the Santa suit. He was holding up a ticket and looking around the room.

"Oh, my heavens!" shouted Iola. She waved her arms in the air. "That's me! I'm Iola Jenkins, and I'm right here!"

Later—much later—when the punch bowl was empty and the record player had been silenced and the band had packed up and gone home, Elmer carried the turkey out of the VFW and heaved it into the back seat of the Pontiac.

"I think they might be telling the truth," he said. "I think it might be the largest turkey in the world." He was breathing hard. "I almost couldn't carry it."

They all got in the car — Beverly in the driver's seat, Iola up front next to her, and Elmer in back with the turkey. On the drive home, Iola hummed "Have Yourself a Merry Little Christmas" several times in a row. And then she said, "Now both of you children know how to dance. Ain't that something?"

"Right," said Beverly. "It's something, I guess."

"Just imagine," said Iola. She reached over and patted Beverly's leg. "Imagine if you hadn't found my trailer. Imagine if I didn't need someone to drive the Pontiac. Then me and you wouldn't've become friends, and you wouldn't know how to dance. Oh, I'm glad I needed you. I'm glad you needed me."

"I didn't really need you," said Beverly.

"Yes, you did, honey," said Iola.

"Yes, you did," said Elmer from the back seat.

"Okay," said Beverly. "Whatever you people say."

When they got to the Seahorse Court, Elmer lifted the turkey out of the back seat and started up the stairs to the trailer. He said, "I hope the world's largest turkey fits through the door of this tiny trailer."

He was halfway up the stairs when Iola called out, "Wait, honey."

"Wait?" said Elmer. He turned around and looked at her. He was holding the turkey low in his arms.

"Well, I just thought: now, where in the world am I going to put that bird? It surely won't fit in my refrigerator."

"Let's try," said Elmer. He turned and started back up the stairs.

"Oh, no, honey. Don't bother. The more I think about it, the more I know I am right. That turkey won't fit. I know that refrigerator. And not only that, I doubt it will fit in the oven. It's a small oven."

"Good grief," said Elmer. He turned again. "It's heavy. Hurry up and tell me where to go."

"Put it on the steps," said Beverly.

"The steps?" said Iola. "We can't leave a turkey setting on the steps. The raccoons will get it."

"I can't hold it anymore," said Elmer. He started to laugh.

"Oh, don't laugh," said Iola. "Now, don't you dare start laughing." She started laughing, too.

Beverly laughed with them.

"Oh no, oh no," said Elmer, still laughing. He walked to the top of the steps. He leaned his head against the door. "I can't," he said.

"Wheeeeee," said Iola.

"Elmer," said Beverly.

He turned and looked at her, and the turkey slid out of his arms and went bouncing down the steps and landed on the grass.

Iola whooped. She bent over and held on to the lawn chair and laughed and laughed.

The turkey sat at the bottom of the steps, and Elmer stood at the top, laughing and wheezing. His tie was loose. His shirt was unbuttoned. His face was lit up.

"It is," he said, "the world's largest . . . turkey."

Beverly sat down on the ground and laughed until she cried.

A light went on in the trailer next to Iola's.

Maureen opened her door. Her red hair was in curlers. She had on a nightgown.

"What's going on out there?" she shouted. "Iola?"

"Wheeeeee," said Iola.

"World's largest turkey," said Elmer to Maureen. He pointed at the turkey. "Won't fit," he said. He pointed at Iola's trailer door. And then he started laughing again.

"Should I call the police?" said Maureen.

"No, no, no," said Iola. She stood up straight. She wiped at the tears on her face. "It's funny is all. I won the turkey at the VFW, and we don't have a place to put it. It's too big."

"It won't fit," said Elmer.

Maureen stood with her hands on her hips. "It's 11:47 p.m.," she said.

"Is it?" said Iola.

"Decent people are asleep," said Maureen.

"We're decent," said Elmer. "But the turkey will not fit." He looked very serious. He was trying hard not to laugh.

Maureen slammed her door.

"Well, what are we going to do now?" said Iola.

"I have an idea," said Beverly.

Thirty-three

The four of them — Beverly, Iola, Elmer, and the turkey — got back in the Pontiac. They drove to Mr. C's.

Beverly went around to the back. She knocked on the kitchen door. No one answered. She knocked harder, and the door slowly opened to reveal Doris.

"I was hoping you were still here," said Beverly.

"Well, I was hoping not to be," said Doris. "But here I am."

"Can I put something in the refrigerator?" said Beverly.

Doris narrowed her eyes. "What is it?"

"The world's largest turkey," said Beverly.

Iola walked up and stood to the right of Beverly. She was holding her purse in both hands.

"Hello," she said.

"Who are you?" said Doris.

"I'm Iola Jenkins. I'm the one who won the turkey."

"This is Doris," said Beverly.

"I'm very pleased to meet you," said Iola.

"Okay," said Doris.

And then Elmer came staggering around the corner with the turkey in his arms.

"Oh, I don't think so," said Doris.

"I told you it was big," said Beverly.

Doris stared at Elmer and the turkey.

"It's heavy," he said to her.

"It sure looks that way," said Doris.

"Please?" said Elmer.

Doris opened the door wider, and Elmer walked into Mr. C's.

"Come on over here with it," said Doris. She opened the door to the walk-in refrigerator, and Elmer, grunting and sweating, went inside with the turkey.

Beverly looked around the kitchen. Charles was asleep on the floor. His legs were curled up, and he had an apron underneath his head for a pillow. His knit cap was still on his head.

Elmer came out of the refrigerator. "Thank you," he said to Doris.

"I know you," she said. "You work down at Zoom City."

"Yes, ma'am," said Elmer.

"I've seen you. Handing out dimes so that the children can ride on that horse."

"Yes, ma'am," said Elmer. He looked at Beverly, and then he looked away.

"Yep," said Doris, nodding. "I know who you are."

"We surely do thank you for the use of the refrigerator," said Iola. "They said down at the VFW that the turkey is already thawed, so I suppose next I need to figure out how to cook it."

Mr. Denby came into the kitchen. "Beverly Anne," he said, "what are you doing here?"

Mr. Denby had on a striped pair of pajamas.

"Hello, Mr. Denby," said Beverly.

"Who are all you people?" said Mr. Denby.

Doris turned to Iola and said, "You're going to need a big oven to cook that bird."

"I know it," said Iola. "I've never cooked a turkey that big in my life. And truth be told, I am a little overwhelmed by the prospect."

"Well, I can tell you what I would do," said Doris. She beckoned to Iola. "Come over here and we will talk it through."

"Will somebody please tell me what is going on?" said Mr. Denby.

Charles sat up. He rubbed his eyes and adjusted his cap. "I was dreaming about something good," he said, "but I don't remember what."

"Maybe we should cook the turkey here," said Elmer. "Maybe we need to cook the turkey and have a big Christmas dinner."

"Christmas?" said Charles.

"What are you talking about?" said Doris.

"It was just Christmas down at the VFW," said Iola.

"Let's keep on having it be Christmas," said Beverly.

"I do love Christmas dinner," said Doris. "Mashed potatoes and gravy."

"And stuffing," said Charles.

"And pie," said Beverly.

Elmer reached out and grabbed her hand, right there in front of everybody.

She let him.

The lights in the kitchen were bright.

"I love pie," said Charles. "But you got to have fruitcake, too."

Elmer swung Beverly's hand back and forth.

"I don't have everything I need here," said Doris. "I'll make up a list, and you all can go and get it."

"All right, then," said Iola.

Mr. Denby put his hands on top of his head. "Can this all stop?" he said. "I'm willing to pay you more, Doris. And you, too, Charles."

"And give us sick days," said Doris. "And do it all proper."

"And give you sick days," said Mr. Denby. "And, yes, do it all proper."

"First," said Doris, "we're going to have Christmas dinner, and after that we can sit and talk about what's fair. What do you think?" she said, turning to Iola. "Can we be ready by four?"

"Let's say five. It's an awfully big bird."

"Five p.m.," said Doris. "Mr. C's stays closed again today."

"Oh, no," said Mr. Denby, "please."

"Also," said Doris to Mr. Denby, "you are in charge of pie."

"And fruitcake," said Charles.

"Where am I going to get a fruitcake this time of year?" said Mr. Denby. He pulled at his hair.

"You'll figure it out," said Doris. "Now, let's make us a big list." She pulled a stool up to the table. Iola sat down next to Doris.

Charles lay back down. He pulled his hat over his eyes.

"But where am I going to get a fruitcake?" said Mr. Denby in a small voice.

No one answered him.

And Beverly and Elmer stood in Mr. C's big kitchen under the bright lights, still holding hands.

Beverly could not stop smiling.

Thirty-four

Before she went to sleep that night, Iola came out to the porch and gave Beverly Elmer's drawing.

"It will always have the crease, I suppose," said Iola. "But it's yours, and you should keep it, honey."

Beverly stared down at the picture.

"What?" said Iola.

"Is that really how I look?" Beverly asked.

"Yes, darling," said Iola. "That is really how you look. Beautiful, like that. Now take it. It's yours."

* * *

That night, Beverly dreamed that she was lying on the ground by Buddy's grave—in the backyard, underneath the orange trees. When she looked up, she saw that the trees were bare. There were no leaves on them at all and no fruit.

Now we'll have to cut them down for sure, thought Beverly. *Now, there is no point.*

She heard the rustle of wings. She looked up. Hovering above the dead orange trees was an angel. Her wings were brown, not blue.

She floated above the trees, looking down at Beverly and the grave.

"What?" said Beverly.

The angel shook her head. She kept opening and closing her mouth. She flapped her brown wings. Why weren't the wings blue? Where was the lapis lazuli?

"What?" said Beverly to the angel again.

And then, in the dream, it started to snow—big swirling flakes.

The snow fell on Buddy's grave, and on the branches of the tree, and on the brown wings of the angel.

The angel kept opening and closing her mouth.

"What did you come to say?" said Beverly.

But the angel didn't speak, and soon everything—the trees, the grass, the grave—was covered in snow.

"What's the message?" Beverly shouted. "Tell me!"

The angel smiled down at Beverly.

The world was radiant with the light from the falling snow.

Beverly woke up to the smell of coffee and the sound of Iola talking.

She put on a pair of jeans and got up and went into the kitchen. A man was sitting at the little table. His hair was slicked back, and his shoes were shined. He was wearing a suit.

"Tommy," said Iola, "this is Beverly."

The man looked directly at Beverly. She looked back. Neither one of them said anything.

"Now, remember your manners. Both of you," said Iola. "Tommy is my oldest son, honey."

"Hi," said Beverly.

"You're the one driving my mother's car?" said Tommy. He drummed his fingers on the tabletop.

"Yeah," said Beverly. "Because your mother asked me to."

"You're just a kid," said Tommy.

"Maureen called Tommy and told him that something crazy was going on over here last night," said Iola. "And now Tommy is worried. That's all. He's just worried."

"That's right," said Tommy. "I'm worried."

"There is nothing to worry about, honey. I told you. We all went to a dance at the VFW last night, and I won the world's largest turkey. That's all that happened."

"Who are you?" Tommy said to Beverly.

"Honey," said Iola, "I just told you. She's Beverly."

"This is the thing, Ma," said Tommy. "I just don't know if I can trust you. You're letting strangers come into your house and live with you. I'm starting to doubt your decision-making skills." He drummed his fingers on the table some more.

"I make excellent decisions," said Iola. She looked very, very small. "Honey, today is our Christmas dinner. Don't ruin it for me."

"See? That's what I'm talking about. Today is not Christmas. It's August, Ma. Not December." Tommy looked at Beverly. "You need to be out of here," he said to her.

"No," said Iola.

"In a week's time," said Tommy. "Or else I take the car."

"You can't do that," said Beverly.

"Sure I can. This is my mother we're talking about. I'm her son. Who are you to tell me what I can and can't do? Huh? Who are you?"

Beverly just stood there.

"Who are you?" said Tommy. "Huh?"

Who was she?

She was someone who used to have a dog. She was someone whose father had held her hand. She was someone who had held Elmer's hand and danced with him. She was someone who was friends with Raymie. And Louisiana—still—even though she was far away. She was someone who had written *I am properly sorry* five hundred times, and didn't mean it once. She was someone who had written Iola's name eighty-two times, and meant it every time. She was someone who had dug a hole and buried someone she loved. She was someone who knew what lapis lazuli was, and that you could grind it up and turn it into wings.

She was someone who wanted things to be different from how they were.

She was someone who wanted things to change.

"See?" said Tommy when she didn't answer him. "You're nobody."

"Don't say that," said Iola. "Don't you tell her that."

Tommy spread his arms wide. "Ma," he said, "I'm trying to take care of you. That's all."

"I can take care of myself. Your daddy would be so . . . so *disappointed* in you, Tommy. He would."

"Yeah, well, Dad's gone," said Tommy. "I make the decisions now."

Iola cried after he left. She sat at the little table with her head in her hands and cried and cried.

Beverly sat across from her. She said, "I don't care, Iola. It's fine. I can't stay here forever anyway."

"I care," said Iola. "And I always knew that you was going to leave. I knew that would happen no matter what. It's just that it was so much fun. Having you here was fun."

Nod hopped up on the table and sat down in between them.

"You stupid cat," said Beverly.

Nod started purring.

"I'm sorry," said Beverly.

"So am I, honey," said Iola. "But I guess there's no point in sitting here crying all day, is there? Get me my purse. You and me are going to go shopping for Christmas dinner."

They went to Muskie Market and walked down the aisles together. Iola pushed the cart. The lights were bright, and the air-conditioning and the freezers and the refrigerators made so much noise that you couldn't hear the ocean, which was kind of a relief.

They got green beans and sweet potatoes and regular potatoes and celery. They got cranberries in a can and onions and bread. They got butter.

"I think I'll make some ambrosia," said Iola. "Do you like ambrosia?"

"What is it?" said Beverly.

"Well, for heaven's sake," said Iola. "I'll just make it for you, and you'll find out. Get me some of them itty-bitty marshmallows and some oranges. And maraschino cherries. And let me think on what else I want to put in there."

She stood with her hands on the cart and stared out into space. Her glasses winked in the overhead light. She was so small.

Beverly put her hand on top of Iola's. "I'll come and visit you," she said.

"Of course you will, darling," said Iola. "I know that." She kept staring off into space. She blinked. "Get me some coconut," she said finally.

"Marshmallows, oranges, maraschino cherries, and coconut. Is that it?" said Beverly.

Iola blinked again. "And also pecans. I believe I'll put some pecans in there. We need to make it the best ambrosia ever, just so you'll know how good it can be."

"Okay," said Beverly. "I already believe it's good."

"Honey," said Iola, "you will be amazed." She looked up at Beverly and smiled. "It is just the best thing, the best and sweetest thing there is."

Thirty-five

They brought all the groceries to Mr. C's.

Doris immediately set Charles to work chopping things, and Beverly went back to Mr. Denby's office.

He was dressed and wearing a tie that didn't have a fish on it. His hair was combed, and he was sitting at his desk and sorting through papers. The little fan was plugged in, twirling back and forth at his feet.

"Merry Christmas," Beverly said to him.

"Right," he said.

"Here," said Beverly. She handed him the photo of the Denby family Christmas.

"What's this?" He squinted at the picture.

"It's you," she said. "Being happy. It was in the safe. I took it. I borrowed it for a while. I'm sorry. I'm giving it back."

Mr. Denby stared at the photograph as if he had never seen it before.

"Look how small Anne was," he said finally. "And look, Margaret's tooth is missing." He reached out and touched each of the girls' faces one by one.

"And that's your wife?" said Beverly.

"Yes." He put the picture down on the desk. He sighed.

"That's when you were all in Pennsylvania together?"

"Yes," said Mr. Denby. "That's correct. Thank you for returning it."

"Mr. Denby—" she said.

A scream came from the kitchen. It sounded like Iola.

"What now?" said Mr. Denby.

And then somebody was standing at the door to Mr. Denby's office. It was a man wearing a ski mask and a tank top, carrying a baseball bat.

"This is a stickup," the masked man said.

"A what?" said Mr. Denby.

"Jerome?" said Beverly.

"Yeah?" said Jerome, turning toward her.

"Is that a Wiffle bat?" she said.

"Yeah?" said Jerome. "So what? Give me all the money in the safe, or else I'll bash your heads in."

"With a Wiffle bat?" said Beverly.

"This doesn't seem right," said Mr. Denby.

"Hurry up, hurry up," said Jerome. He waved the bat through the air. It made a swishing noise.

"Let's all just be calm," said Mr. Denby.

"I am calm," said Jerome. "I'm real calm. Give me the money—all the money in the safe. Put it in here." He held out a paper grocery sack.

"I have three daughters," said Mr. Denby. "This money is not my money to give away."

"That's the truth," said Doris. She was standing in the doorway to the office with her arms crossed.

Iola was behind her, and behind Iola, Beverly could see Charles's green knit cap.

"Give me the money!" shouted Jerome. He swung the Wiffle bat down on the orange chair. It made a sad-sounding thwack.

"Just give him the money, Mr. Denby," said Beverly.

"But that's not fair," said Mr. Denby.

"Don't you give him that money," said Doris.

"Is that a Wiffle bat?" said Charles.

"I will hurt somebody!" shouted Jerome. "I promise I will hurt somebody."

Mr. Denby turned to the safe. He picked up the stacks of bills and put them in the grocery bag that Jerome was holding out to him. "This is not right," said Mr. Denby. "This is not right at all."

Jerome turned around. "Move," he said to Doris.

"No," she said.

"Move!" He raised the bat.

Iola put her hand on Doris's shoulder. "Step back, honey," she said. "Let him go."

Jerome went out the door of the office, and then he turned back and looked right at Beverly.

He took off the ski mask. He said, "If you call the cops, I'll come back here to this stupid fish place and break everybody's bones. I promise you I will."

And then he was gone. Beverly heard the kitchen door slam.

"Call the police!" said Iola.

"No," said Mr. Denby.

"I'll get him," said Beverly.

Charles said, "You take the front door. I'll take the back."

Beverly went out the front door of Mr. C's and into the bright light. She blinked. Jerome's truck was sitting in the parking lot.

The engine was running, and Freddie was in the driver's seat. She was looking at herself in the rearview mirror. She was applying mascara.

Beverly went over to the truck and knocked on the window. Freddie jumped.

Beverly made the gesture to roll down the window.

Freddie looked all around the empty parking lot, and then she slowly rolled down the window.

"What do you want?" she said.

"I think you're supposed to be out back," said Beverly.

Freddie blinked. "Why?" she said.

"Because that's the door that Jerome went out of," said Beverly. "With the money."

"Are you sure?" said Freddie.

"Yep," said Beverly. "I'm sure." She smiled. "Anyway, I think you might be too late. Charles— you know Charles, broken Charles, Charles who used to play football?—he's out back. He's probably already caught Jerome."

Freddie slammed the truck into reverse and went screeching out of the parking lot.

Beverly stood there for a minute, still smiling.

It was hot.

She could smell the ocean and fried fish and exhaust. And underneath that, there was the smell of something else. What was it?

Turkey.

Christmas.

Doris and Iola must have put the turkey in the oven.

Beverly walked back behind Mr. C's. She went

past the kitchen and headed down to the water. She saw Charles's cap—green against the blue. She walked closer and saw that Jerome was facedown in the sand. Charles was sitting on top of him, smiling.

He saw Beverly. He took his hat off and waved to her. "I got him!" he shouted. "I got him."

"Good!" she shouted back. She stood and stared at the water, and at Charles sitting on top of Jerome, and suddenly, what Beverly wanted more than anything else in the world was to see Elmer's face.

She turned around. She put her back to the ocean and headed up to the road. She turned left and started walking down A1A in the direction of Zoom City.

She walked past the phone booth, and then she turned and went back.

She opened the door and went inside.

Thirty-six

The phone on the other end rang once, twice, three times.

"Hello?" said Raymie.

Beverly closed her eyes. She squeezed them shut. She was working to keep the tears in.

"Hello?" said Raymie again.

Beverly opened her eyes. "Remember when Louisiana disappeared?" she said.

"Beverly," said Raymie, "where are you?"

"Remember how we went looking through the whole house," said Beverly, "and there was this one room where the window was open and the window shade was kind of moving back and forth, back and forth in the wind?" She could feel the tears sliding down her cheeks.

"I guess so," said Raymie. "Where are you?"

"That was the loneliest feeling in the world," said Beverly.

"It was terrible," said Raymie.

"I hated it. It was as bad as Buddy dying. It was as bad as my father leaving." The tears were rolling off her face and falling onto her arms. She said, "I'm sorry. I'm sorry I left without telling you anything. I wrote you a letter."

"I never got a letter."

"That's because I haven't mailed it yet."

"I keep looking for you," said Raymie. "And I go to Buddy's grave. Every day since you left, I've gone back there."

"Oh," said Beverly. She started to cry even harder.

"Where are you?" asked Raymie again.

"Maybe you could come and get me," said Beverly.

Raymie was quiet.

Something on the line crackled.

"Hello?" said Beverly.

"Tell me where you are," said Raymie.

Beverly told her.

And then she hung up the phone and wiped the tears off her face. She tilted her head so that she could see the words scratched in the glass.

In a crooked little house by a crooked little sea.

She stepped out of the phone booth and started walking toward Zoom City. Before she even got there, she could hear the horse—the creak and grind of it moving up and down. She stopped and just listened to it, the noise of something laboring to go nowhere. She held herself very still.

And then she walked up to the store and looked at the kid on the horse. It was Robbie. The boy from the beach, the sandcastle kid.

"Hey!" he said. He stood with his feet in the stirrups. He pointed at Beverly. "You lied. You said you would come back, and you didn't come back.

We were going to finish that castle, but you never showed up."

"Sit down, Robbie," said his mother.

"I'll be right back," said Beverly.

"Liar!" said Robbie.

Beverly opened the door of Zoom City. She stuck her head inside. Mr. Larksong was at the counter.

Elmer looked up at her. He smiled.

"Hi," she said. "We had a little bit of excitement down at Mr. C's, but everything is fine. Everything worked out. I just wanted to remind you that we're going to be eating soon. Why don't you come, too, Mr. Larksong? There's going to be a lot of food. It's Christmas."

"Christmas?" said Mr. Larksong. "It's Christmas?"

"Yep," said Beverly. "It is."

She turned and went back outside. Robbie was still on the horse.

"I'm sorry," she said to him. "I'm sorry I didn't show up."

She wondered if she was going to spend all day just apologizing to people.

"I don't care," said Robbie.

"Don't be rude, Robbie," said his mother.

"Do you like pie?" Beverly asked Robbie.

"What kind?" said Robbie. He narrowed his eyes.

"I think there's going to be pumpkin. And apple. And maybe fruitcake. We're having a big dinner down at Mr. C's."

"That's a fish place," said Robbie. "I hate fish."

"Yeah," said Beverly. "Me, too. But this isn't a fish dinner. There's going to be turkey. And something called ambrosia, which has got marshmallows in it." She looked at Robbie's mother. "It's kind of a Christmas dinner. Mr. C's is just down the street, if you want to—I don't know—drop in or something."

The horse creaked to a stop. Robbie sat and stared at her.

"See you around, okay?" she said.

And then she walked away from Zoom City. She thought that if Mrs. Deely popped out of the bushes, she would invite her to Christmas dinner, too. Maybe she would invite everyone she met.

* * *

When she got back to Mr. C's, she went around back. The kitchen door was propped open, and the seagull was standing there—staring inside.

She stood with him. She stared inside, too.

Iola and Doris and Mr. Denby and Charles were all working in the kitchen.

Iola looked up and saw her first. She said, "There you are. I wondered where you got to. Charles caught that robber, caught him and got all the money back."

"I know it," said Beverly. "I saw it. It was heroic. Um, I invited some more people."

"Well, that's good," said Iola. "That's exactly what Christmas is all about."

Beverly suddenly remembered that Raymie was on her way.

And Elmer, of course.

They would both be here soon.

Her heart lifted. Something inside of her fluttered. She turned and looked behind her. The sun was shining on the sea.

The crooked little sea.

"Get in here," said Doris. "There's work to do."

The seagull lifted his wings. He let out a hopeful squawk.

"Not you," said Doris. "I'm not talking to you."

The seagull lowered his wings, and Beverly Tapinski carefully stepped around him.

She went inside.

Kate DiCamillo is the beloved author of many books for young readers, including two Newbery Medal winners: *The Tale of Despereaux* and *Flora & Ulysses*. She grew up in Florida and moved to Minnesota in her twenties, where homesickness and a bitter winter led her to write her first published novel, *Because of Winn-Dixie*. It was named a Newbery Honor Book, and she followed it with many other award-winning books, including two #1 *New York Times* best-selling novels about the Three Rancheros.

Kate DiCamillo was selected to be the National Ambassador for Young People's Literature for 2014–2015. Of that mission, and on the power of stories, she says, "When we read together, we connect. Together, we see the world. Together, we see one another."

For discussion guides and other resources
for Kate DiCamillo's books, please visit
www.KateDiCamilloStoriesConnectUs.com.

Follow Kate DiCamillo on Facebook
at **Facebook.com/KateDiCamillo.**

Don't miss the #1 *New York Times* bestseller, now featuring a stunning new cover!

#1 NEW YORK TIMES BEST-SELLING AUTHOR

KATE DiCAMILLO

RAYMIE NIGHTINGALE

HC: 978-0-7636-8117-3 • PB: 978-0-7636-9691-7
Also available as an e-book

Raymie Clarke has a plan. If she can win the Little Miss Central Florida Tire competition, then her father, who left town two days ago with a dental hygienist, will see Raymie's picture in the paper and (maybe) come home. To win, not only does Raymie have to do good deeds and learn how to twirl a baton; she also has to contend with the wispy, frequently fainting Louisiana Elefante and the fiery, stubborn Beverly Tapinski.

From two-time Newbery Medalist Kate DiCamillo comes a #1 *New York Times* bestseller about discovering who you are—and deciding who you want to be.

HC: 978-0-7636-9463-0
Also available as an e-book

When Granny wakes her up in the middle of the night to tell her that the day of reckoning has arrived and they have to leave home immediately, Louisiana isn't overly worried. After all, Granny has many middle-of-the-night ideas. But this time, things are different. This time, Granny intends for them never to return.

More from Kate DiCamillo

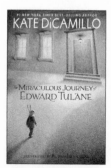

A Newbery
Honor Book

A National Book
Award Finalist

Winner of the
Newbery Medal

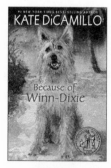

A #1 *New York
Times* Bestseller

A *New York
Times* Bestseller

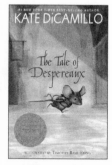

Winner of the
Newbery Medal

www.candlewick.com